PU

LITTLE YEAR

Thirteen years old . . . hig
going to be a successful human being, become *somebody*
before it's too late.

When Mrs da Susa, Lord Willoughby's Deputy Head, organizes the first Addendon Children's Book Fair at the school, Annabel is waiting to impress the visiting publishers with her collected poems – that is, until her own ambitions become submerged in a still greater cause; the future of her favourite author's books and, in Annabel's view, of English literature itself.

And in the second of these two stories, Annabel embarks on a series of desperate attempts to get into the Guinness Book of Records. It is, she tells Kate, the only answer; to do something dramatic to make her mark in life *now*. But, wonders Kate, the answer to *what*, exactly?

Annabel's yearnings prove to be both touching and extremely funny in this latest volume of stories about Alan Davidson's very popular and original heroine.

Also published in Puffin are *A FRIEND LIKE ANNABEL*, *JUST LIKE ANNABEL*, *EVEN MORE LIKE ANNABEL* and *THE NEW, THINKING ANNABEL*. Alan Davidson lives in Dorset and is also the author of *THE BEWITCHING OF ALISON ALLBRIGHT*.

ALAN DAVIDSON

*****

Little yearnings of Annabel

PUFFIN BOOKS

PUFFIN BOOKS

Published by the Penguin Group
27 Wrights Lane, London w 8 5 t z, England
Viking Penguin Inc., 40 West 23rd Street, New York,
New York 10010, USA
Penguin Books Australia Ltd, Ringwood, Victoria, Australia
Penguin Books Canada Ltd, 2801 John Street, Markham,
Ontario, Canada l 3 r 1 b 4
Penguin Books (NZ) Ltd, 182–190 Wairau Road, Auckland 10,
New Zealand

Penguin Books Ltd, Registered Offices: Harmondsworth,
Middlesex, England

First published by Grafton Books 1986
Published in Puffin Books 1989
1 3 5 7 9 10 8 6 4 2

Made and printed in Great Britain by
Cox and Wyman Ltd, Reading, Berks.
Filmset in Linotron Trump Medieval by
Rowland Phototypesetting Ltd
Bury St Edmunds, Suffolk

To Anne and David Stokes

Contents

*****

Annabel
and the Addendon
Children's Book Fair

*****

Chapter 1

*****

'It is going to be,' said Kate, reading from the programme, 'a feast of children's literature, a rich and exciting brew of books, authors, artists, reviewers and publishers. Jim Troops, author of the prize-winning *Pit Mates*, which reveals the viciousness of eighteenth century Yorkshire coal owners, will be here. So will – are you listening, Annabel?'

'Mildly,' said Annabel. She was lying full-length on the floor of her bedroom, resting on her elbows and turning the pages of a little stiff-backed notebook which lay on the floor in front of her. Kate was sitting on the bed.

'– so will Sheila Carew-Singlesmith whose much-acclaimed books about Pitts Road School revealing what life's really like in a tough inner-city comprehensive are shortly to be televised and Martin Mulloon who, in his books, reveals the dilemmas which confront a young girl growing up . . . I suppose Mrs da Susa wrote all this stuff, did she, Annabel?'

'I expect so. I expect she copied it from other people's programmes.'

'Imagine!' Kate turned the pages. 'All this going on at Willers.'

'It's the publishers I'm interested in, Kate.'

Annabel Bunce (13 – address: 9 Badger's Close, Addendon – education: in progress at Lord Willoughby's School, class 3 G) and her best friend Kate Stocks (13 – address: 14 Oakwood Crescent, Addendon – education: ditto) had known for some time that Mrs da Susa, Deputy Head of Lord Willoughby's, was organizing the first Addendon Children's Book Fair, to be held at the school; could hardly have failed to know because she had been in a state of tremulous excitement about it for some weeks, referring to it constantly in R.E. Now, a few days before the event, the programme had become available.

'Oh! – and Annabel – the author of the Connie Cauliflower books is coming.'

'*Connie Cauliflower!*' Annabel woke up. She scrambled to her knees. 'You're not teasing, are you, Kate?'

'Why should I be teasing? It says so here at the bottom of the back page.'

'T. P. Roseland?'

'Yes.'

Annabel rose and, closing her little book, placed it on the dressing-table. It was a book containing the best of all the poems she had ever written and been able to find or remember, printed out as neatly and attractively as she could manage. She had made a dust jacket for it and covered it with a lovingly executed design of flowers and butterflies, all beautifully coloured in. It was as nearly like a real book as she could make it with the materials at her disposal. The title, in stick-on letters, was modest, restrained, prestigious:

ANNABEL FIDELITY BUNCE
COLLECTED POEMS

She had been working on it ever since first hearing about the Book Fair, sorting out old forgotten poems in backs of exercise books, polishing them up, adding a few new ones. Mrs da Susa's Book Fair was a not-to-be-missed opportunity to show them to a publisher. She wasn't sure of their worth but she had hopes and, anyway, she might at least get some opinions and criticism which would be of help in the future. As she'd said to Kate with a modest little smile, 'it would be a pity

> To be a great poet
> And never to know it

because you'd never shown your work to anyone.'

Mention of Connie Cauliflower and T. P. Roseland drove all that from her mind for the moment.

'T. P. Roseland! In Addendon! I can't believe it, Kate. Let me see.'

It was just one sentence in a little *Stop Press* section at the foot of the back page: *T. P. Roseland, author of the Connie Cauliflower books, will be attending the Fair.*

'It's like hearing that King Arthur's coming, Kate. A legend. I've never thought of T. P. Roseland as being a real person living somewhere just like anybody else, though I suppose he must be if you think about it . . . if T. P. Roseland *is* a he. Is it a he, Kate?'

'I don't know.'

'I think it's probably a he. I've got a picture in my mind. Somebody larger than life and smiling and jolly but not, absolutely not, just an ordinary person. Have you read the Connie Cauliflower books, Kate?'

'No. I missed out on them, somehow. I always meant to.'

'You should have. I can't think why I haven't made you.' Annabel went to her bookcase and pulled out a row of books, jammed together between her hands, their covers dog-eared from reading and re-reading. 'Nothing, Kate, absolutely nothing, has had a greater influence on my life than Connie Cauliflower. I think it would be fair to say, Kate, that it's the example of Connie Cauliflower that's made me what I am today.'

Kate glanced at the first book. It was all about the adventures of Connie and her many friends: shy, introverted Cedric Cabbage; fat, chuckling lie-abed Monty Marrow; thin, sniffing, lugubrious lie-abed Charlie Cucumber, Parson Parsnip, Mr Leek the schoolmaster and their glamorous acquaintances from the flower beds such as Jolly Polly Anthus and Sweet William.

There was a picture of Connie Cauliflower on the cover, a sweetly smiling cauliflower head wearing a charming collar of green leaves. She wasn't glamorous, far from it, but she more than made up for this by being sweet and kind and always coming up with a superb wheeze when any of her friends was in trouble – which they invariably were – with one of their enemies such as the Great Evil Weevil or the sinister Doctor Blight. That was partly why they all loved her so much.

The garden where they lived was a happy place, more sweetly-scented, more butterfly- and dragonfly-haunted, more filled with the summery droning of bees than any ordinary garden and all presided over by a kindly gardener who talked and sang to his plants because he thought they liked it, which indeed they did. They liked it *very* much.

'It doesn't say if he'll be doing anything special at the Fair, does it, Kate. Some of the other authors are giving talks or drawing pictures or telling jokes.'

'Signing books, probably.'

'Being in the *stop press* means they didn't know he was coming till the last moment. Probably had to persuade him. Must be a bit of a triumph for Mrs da Susa.' Annabel sat down beside Kate then got up again, too excited to remain still. 'I wonder when he'll arrive and where he'll be staying?'

'Three Tuns, I expect. And probably arriving at Querminster station on Thursday afternoon, the train from London that gets in at 4.12. Most of the important guests are coming then, aren't they, in time for Mrs da Susa's wine and cheese party at six o'clock.'

This was common knowledge at Lord Willoughby's by now as Annabel herself would have remembered if she hadn't been so wrapped up in her poems. Also known was that several teachers would be offering accommodation to guests.

Mrs da Susa, for instance, would have staying with her those two influential book reviewers Ms Maureen Marone and Ms Mollie Pike (Annabel had every intention that both these ladies should see her poems) while Mrs Jesty and her husband would be giving hospitality to Jim Troops, the author. The publishers would not be taking advantage of this charity but would be staying at Addendon's only proper hotel, the Three Tuns. Perhaps, it had been surmised, they had better expense accounts.

'4.12 on Thursday. The day we break up for half-term. I shall be at the station to see him, Kate.'

'Oh, Annabel! All you'll see of him there is getting into a car to be driven to Addendon. You may as well wait till the next day and see him properly. Still supposing it *is* a he.'

'I'm afraid, Kate, that I can't wait that long.' Annabel sat down on the bed again and this time stayed there, hands clasped in her lap. 'I'm trying to imagine it . . . T. P. Roseland at Willers. Treading the same corridors that we tread, sniffing the same smells that we sniff . . . old school dinners and furniture polish . . . strange, uncouth words passing his lips like – like *Addendon* and *Mrs da Susa* . . .

Mrs Bunce was calling up the stairs that it was supper time. Kate got up to go.

'I'm trying, Kate, but it's hard. Will it really happen on Thursday?'

Today was Monday. It was an achingly long time to wait.

Lord Willoughby's broke up for half-term at noon on Thursday. At four o'clock that afternoon a welcoming party from the school assembled on Platform 2 at Querminster station to await the arrival of the train from London.

The welcoming party – each member of which wore an *Addendon Children's Book Fair* badge on his or her clothing to ease identification – was composed of the four leading members of the Book Fair committee: Mrs da Susa, Deputy Head of Lord Willoughby's and Head of English (Chair); Mrs Jesty, history (Secretary), Mr Toogood, also of the English department and Mr Ribbons, the Far Left Wing physics teacher (committee members).

Mrs da Susa was, naturally, in a state of nervous excitement. This was the first book fair she had ever organized and she was, of course, keen that it should be a memorable one and go without a hitch. In the first of these two aims, at any rate, she was not to be disappointed, as will be seen.

Standing at some distance from the official welcoming party and concealed from it by the station bookstall was a second, unofficial one. Annabel, accompanied by Kate, had been there since soon after three and was clutching a new autograph book, new because she wanted the name of T. P. Roseland to adorn the first page. It was Annabel's intention to seize upon him the moment he got off the train, stick the autograph book under his nose and rapidly tell him of her devotion to his work before the official party could get to him.

'But you won't know which is him,' Kate had protested. 'You're not even sure it's a man. You're only guessing.'

'I shall know,' Annabel had replied with calm certainty. 'Once I see him – or her, it's not important which it is – there will be a communion between us, a bond of understanding. I know that from his – or her – books.'

At 4.26 the train came crawling slowly round the bend and the driver became distinguishable, carefully blowing his nose and clearly oblivious of the momentous and precious cargo he had the honour to be hauling. He drew the train to a halt with infinite gradualness as if trying to show how delicately it could be done and that he didn't care that he was already fourteen minutes late and it was no use anyone carping about it. Just the merest defiant little jolt and the train was at rest, whining gently.

Annabel, who would have liked to go and tap on his window and carp, since she had been kept waiting fourteen minutes longer than was necessary for what might be the most memorable moment of her life, refrained only because to do so might have delayed the moment still longer.

Doors were opening and distinguished members of the publishing profession were stepping out on to the platform.

First amongst them was Jim Troops, casually slamming the door behind him and threatening to break the leg of his publisher, Linda-Jane Gaiters, Editorial Director of Children's Books at Magpie Books PLC, who was just behind him. She withdrew it just in time to the accompaniment of little screams from her publicity assistants, tall, pretty young Nikki Watson and petite, pretty young Nina Jenkins-Tuttle.

She made no protest, however, for in her eyes Jim Troops could do no wrong. True, she had been known to treat him off-handedly in the past but that had been when he was just another struggling author. Now all that was changed. Since the prize-winning *Pit Mates* and subsequent books which, though varied in setting, always displayed a passionate concern for the under-privileged, past, present and future, and for the need for sweeping social change in most countries of the world, he had become very fashionable and profitable. His books were televised, bought hugely by libraries and read in class in schools.

Ms Gaiters was particularly excited by his latest book, due to be published the next day, which she believed to be his most brilliant yet. Finally sweeping aside old outworn conventions and cunningly combining popular appeal with a searing social message it would, she was convinced, open a new chapter in children's

literature, educating its readers in social aware-
ness while making pots of money too. It was the
ultimate and, as she had assured the Chairman of
Magpie Books when requesting funds with which
to promote the book: 'Ted,' (they were on Chris-
tian name terms) 'I know the kids will respond
positively.'

The title of this great book, so far known only
within the trade, would be revealed on publication the following day. Indeed – to divulge a
little secret – the sole reason Ms Gaiters and her
team from Magpie Books had come to Addendon,
a place she had not previously heard of and the
whereabouts of which she was still uncertain,
was because its Book Fair happened to be at
a convenient time at which to launch the
promotion.

In view of all this, she was quite prepared to
tolerate a certain amount of uncouthness on the
part of Jim Troops, even to welcome it as a sign of
genius. She was, in any case, a genuine devotee of
his work which she regarded as central to the
modern predicament.

Jim Troops himself was dressed in a dirty old
blue sweater with holes in the elbows and
patched, dirty old dark blue trousers. No one had
ever seen him in a sweater which didn't have
holes in the elbows so presumably he either cut
them himself or bought them ready holed from
jumble sales in order to maintain his image.
Although now quite wealthy, he lived with his
wife and two small children in a gloomily un-

pleasant terraced house with no bathroom in a dreary part of east London. He said it was his spiritual home although he had actually been brought up in a very comfortable house in Pinner. His wife loathed it but grudgingly accepted it as part of the price of being married to a genius.

On his being introduced, Mr Ribbons nodded approvingly, recognizing a kindred spirit with whom he felt that instinctive *communion* to which Annabel had referred. On the other hand Mrs Jesty, with whom he would be staying and who would have to face him coming out of the bathroom in the mornings, looked rather disconcerted. Being elderly, her mental image of authors was perhaps on the romantic side. A certain bohemianism, a roguish eccentricity of dress and behaviour – this would be acceptable and even enlivening over breakfast and she would be able to tell stories about it afterwards – but Jim Troops was not in that style.

Mrs da Susa wasn't sure about Jim Troops either. She would reserve judgement. About Linda-Jane Gaiters, however, she had no reservations whatever. It was another case of instant *rapport* as she warmly clasped the long, pale hand extended towards her and they exchanged their first words. Linda-Jane Gaiters was a slim, washed-out, haggard-faced person of fading youth in a dress of pale blue and grey alternating stripes. Like Mrs da Susa she was an English graduate – though her degree was a Lower Second from a modern Midlands university while Mrs da Susa's

21

was a First at Oxford – and they recognized intuitively that each would know what the other was talking about when they used phrases like 'the demotic tradition of narrative' and 'the idea of literature as a social construct'.

Mr Ribbons, too, shook Ms Gaiters' hand warmly and glinted his rimless glasses at her, for although Jim Troops was the more obvious soulmate, Ms Gaiters was the one with power to accept manuscripts for publication and, like Annabel, he had a little something of his own up his sleeve.

While all this communing and hand-shaking was going on, Annabel was surveying the dismounted passengers and waiting for a communion of her own, but so far in vain.

'How do you know that he – or she – isn't one of them?' asked Kate, peeping again past the bookstall at the still growing group around Mrs da Susa. 'You *can't* be certain.'

'I can, Kate. I'd know.' Annabel was troubled and disappointed. 'Perhaps he hasn't come on this train, after all.'

The train was standing solidly at the platform, still whining gently and showing no sign of moving although everyone who intended getting on or off appeared to have done so Perhaps the driver had gone into a trance. What seemed to be the last of the distinguished visitors were now joining Mrs da Susa's group amidst a flurry of handshakes and, in a state of flustered, twittering happiness she was about to lead them all to the exit.

'I don't know how you can be,' said Kate. 'What about the one with the funny hat on?'

'I'm afraid, Kate, that you just don't understand at all.'

The one with the funny hat on was, in fact, Maureen Marone, the distinguished critic. She was wearing a full length black dress and a purple hat with a brim so large and flexible that it undulated as she walked, like waves on the sea, giving the impression that she was swimming or sailing everywhere. Ms Marone prided herself on not reviewing books she didn't like while heaping unstinted praise on those she did. Her favourite comment on a book was that it was 'hauntingly beautiful'.

Her uneasy companion on the train had been Mollie Pike, who was now at her side. Ms Pike, in red corduroy trousers and white sweater, affected a straggly hair-style which fell in a threatening fringe almost to her glaring eyes.

This fearsome appearance was belied by her manner, which was meek and giggly. This again was belied by her reviews, which were invariably forthright and often savage, sneering and jeering at the unfortunate work in question before contemptuously tossing it aside. She was not so much concerned with the story, which she hardly noticed, as whether the book pushed back boundaries and swept away outdated literary conventions, of which she assumed there to be a never ending supply, promoted the correct radical values – her own – and employed a language the kids understand and talk amongst themselves'.

This was, apparently, a uniformly snarling, aggressive, vaguely suburban, semi-Americanized, sub-English twang, which ought to have been depressing for Ms Pike since she earned her living as a teacher of English in a north London school, paid to awaken her pupils to an appreciation of the English language as being something better than the sort of stuff that delighted her so much in books ('the author has a keen ear for playground dialogue').

A typical favourable review might read: 'At last something that isn't a load of old gunk. Just the thing to read aloud to your mob in class – if you can face kids as they really are. If you're the sort who objects to bad taste, violence etc., better stick to Enid Blyton.'

Ms Marone she regarded as a silly old bore. Addendon, too, she expected to be a bore. How could people drag out their lives in such places?

Annabel paid her no attention whatsoever.

'What about the man looking lost?' suggested Kate, becoming desperate. 'Don't you get a feeling of communion with him?'

'Don't be silly, Kate. Nor the woman with big teeth.'

The man was Martin Mulloon, the author whose books so sensitively revealed the dilemmas of young girls growing up. He was standing self-consciously to one side in a suit rather too large for his long, lean, slightly stooping figure, hands clasped behind his back as if he didn't know what to do with them. The woman with big teeth was Sheila Carew-Singlesmith, comfortable and dumpy in plain grey suit and cream blouse. Perhaps her teeth weren't really bigger than any-one else's, maybe she just showed more of them in her frequent jolly laughs.

'They're going,' said Kate.

The whole party was now lurching and slouching and undulating towards the station exit.

'He can't have come,' said Annabel, dejected.

'I just don't know how you can be sure,' sighed Kate. But Annabel remained disconsolate, auto-graph book hanging from her hand.

The train still wasn't moving and Kate sud-denly saw why. There was activity at the guard's van. A man was backing out of it, arms round a huge cardboard box which was supported on the other side by the guard. Together they man-oeuvred the box on to the platform and put it down, then the guard hauled a large suitcase out of the van and put that down, too. He stepped back aboard and the train slid away leaving the first man looking about him, presumably for a trolley.

'That's him,' said Annabel, suddenly, and for some reason her eyes filled with tears. 'That's T. P. Roseland.'

He was a tall, well-built man in light grey, faintly checked suit, grey hat and red tie. An umbrella was hooked on to one arm and – what was that dangling on his chest? A monocle! A magazine stuck out of his jacket pocket.

'How can you be sure?'

'I just am.' The tears were still standing in Annabel's eyes. Perhaps they were simply a release of the emotions she felt for the Connie Cauliflower books; for the magical glow they gave her just to think about them; for their warmth and excitement and fun and the way, for her, they enriched the most ordinary of things and made them exciting and beautiful.

With the help of a member of the station staff, the man was now lifting the huge box on to a trolley. Despite her previous scepticism, Kate could see what Annabel meant. Although quite elderly there was a perennially youthful robustness about him. Hat slightly askew, umbrella poking out at an angle, even struggling with the box he managed to radiate a good humour that went with the Connie Cauliflower books.

On the other hand, it couldn't be T. P. Roseland or Mrs da Susa wouldn't have gone off without him.

'What's in the box, anyway?' asked Kate, fascinated. 'It's enormous.'

As if in reply, the bottom of it fell out, followed by the contents. The two men hesitated for a moment, perplexed, then since what remained of the box was now useless, pulled it clear of what was inside. The box had been placed, over the years, on many station platforms and been hoisted on and off countless trolleys. It had been able to take no more and simply disintegrated.

What had fallen out was very large, creamy-white in colour and wearing a collar of green leaves and a modest smile.

It was Connie Cauliflower. Or, to be more precise, a model of her. She bounced and rolled a little then settled on her side, startlingly human in appearance, smiling her sweet smile at the newspaper kiosk while the train, gathering speed, swept past and a dozen people turned to stare.

T. P. Roseland – for there could be no doubt of his identity now – looked down at her still with that faintly perplexed expression on his face. Then, as if needing to convince himself of what he was seeing, he stuck his monocle in his eye.

The first audible reaction came from Annabel. Having remained transfixed for a few moments she emitted an agonized wail.

'Oh, Kate! She might have hurt herself!'

Chapter 2

*****

So horrified was Annabel, so concerned for Connie Cauliflower, that she immediately rushed to inspect her, quite forgetting for the moment that the person she was pushing past to do so was the great, the legendary T. P. Roseland whose very mortality she had been doubtful of till recently. They examined her together; he giving soothing assurances that, although so gentle in appearance, Connie was really very well constructed and tough enough to take much harder knocks than this 'though I must admit I was a little worried for a moment because she's been around for rather a long time now and I think her glue may be deteriorating'; she fussing tenderly, just as if she were Connie's creator and he some sympathetic bystander. The member of the station staff, meanwhile, became impatient and went off to attend to other things.

Only when satisfied about Connie's condition did Annabel remember to become awestruck again. She immediately avoided T. P. Roseland's eye and started mumbling about her autograph book which she'd dropped on the platform, hunting vaguely around for it till Kate pointed out that she was standing on it.

T. P. Roseland promptly invited her and Kate to tea in the buffet.

'I need to park Connie for a minute or two and take stock of the situation.'

He was leaning on his umbrella. His monocle had fallen out of his eye and was dangling on his chest again. 'I've got to get to a place called Addendon. You wouldn't happen to know about buses, would you?'

'We know everything there is to know about Addendon, don't we, Kate.' Annabel was recovering her composure. He was very easy to talk to. He was, after all, a kindred spirit. 'We live there. But –' she suddenly remembered ' – some of our teachers are outside the station with cars. You'd better hurry. You might just catch them.'

'They probably wouldn't welcome transporting Connie.' He didn't look in the least bothered about that, simply continued leaning on his umbrella. 'Lord Willoughby's teachers, you mean. Where the Book Fair's being held. Is that where you go to school?'

The invitation to tea was only just sinking in. Annabel could but nod.

'Lucky I bumped into you. You wouldn't happen to be going back to Addendon soon, would you?'

'Any time. Aren't we, Kate.'

'Perhaps we can go together then and you can give me a hand with Connie. I'd appreciate it if you would. She's light as a feather but awkward for one person. We can stick her outside the buffet for the moment. The box is finished, I'm afraid. I'll squash it up and put it in a bin.'

Annabel had the numb look of one plunged into fantasy.

They left Connie standing outside the door of the buffet treating the whole of Querminster station to her smile and chose a table from which they were able to keep an eye on her. Such was the power of that smile, Kate observed, that several people, having looked startled upon first seeing her, then smiled back. Small children stopped to talk to her and touch her. Connie was spreading sweetness and light over Querminster station in the early rush hour.

Annabel sat in a semi-trance.

'Do you realize, Kate, that these are moments we shall cherish for the rest of our lives. We are taking tea with a genius.'

'But, Annabel, why didn't the others wait for him?'

'They can't have known he was coming on that train, can they, Kate. I suppose he didn't tell them. He doesn't seem to care.'

They were alone at the table. The genius was pushing a tray along in the queue. At the till, he dug deep into his pocket for change and stuck his monocle in his eye, severely distorting one side of his face to do so, while he sorted it out, then picked his way uncertainly towards them, cups and saucers rattling. He'd got them sausage sandwiches which Annabel was not too awestricken to drool over.

'Ridiculous price,' he commented cheerfully as he sat down. Annabel took this to be a light remark, made to help put Kate and her at their ease for of course T. P. Roseland was a millionaire, able to afford unlimited quantities of tea and sausage sandwiches, at any price, if he so wished. Nevertheless, she offered to pay for theirs, at which he laughed and said he hadn't meant to suggest that.

He had an engaging chuckle. Kate noticed that the magazine sticking out of his pocket was to do with vintage cars.

'You could get a new model made, couldn't you, Mr Roseland,' Annabel said, referring back to Connie's glue. 'I expect you're very fond of this one, though. She's very lifelike.'

'I'm extremely fond of her, though there are other considerations, too. Money, for instance. A Connie like that doesn't come cheap. Maybe I could simply get her glue renewed.'

More setting at ease. He probably found his great fame and wealth embarrassing.

'What's the model for, Mr Roseland?' asked Kate. 'What do you do with her?'

'Publicity. You get inside her and walk around. It advertises my books. I take her to as many book fairs as I can. My wife gets a bit stroppy about being left alone so much, actually. She says other people have retired at my age so why can't I.'

'You mean you *wear* her?'

'Not personally. She'd look silly with a pair of

31

Harris tweed trousers sticking out, but I find somebody who will, usually one of my publishers' publicity assistants. Nikki Watson did it last time. They grumble about it – seem to think Connie's a bit scruffy and they've got better things to do – but I remind them they are my publishers whether they like it or not.'

He pointed to the large suitcase which he'd put under the table.

'I bring a supply of my books to sign, too, in case they forget. They usually do.'

Annabel was ignoring his jokes. She was deep in thought and Kate wondered what about. When they'd finished their tea and sausage sandwiches T. P. Roseland looked at his watch.

'Better be moving, I suppose.'

'Yes.' Annabel roused herself. 'You don't want to be late for the wine and cheese party, do you, Mr Roseland.'

'What wine and cheese party?'

'The one at school to welcome all the authors and people.'

'Is there one? Anyway, I'm not invited. I just want to get to Addendon to find some digs and settle in. Perhaps you know of a decent bed and breakfast place, somewhere that wouldn't flinch at the sight of Connie and – er – cheap.'

Annabel couldn't let him get away with that. 'Mrs da Susa would hardly not invite *you*,' she said sceptically.

'I expect they forgot I was coming. Can't blame them – nobody invited me here. I invited myself.

I'm a gate-crasher, I'm afraid. I expect they think I'm a frightful nuisance for being here at all and having to put me in the programme and that I'll get in everybody's way but I'm hardened to that. I'm a very experienced gate-crasher.'

He was clearly the most terrible tease.

'If you're not going to the party,' Annabel pointed out, 'you didn't need to come on this train. There are later ones.'

'Shrewd!' He rose and reached for his hat and umbrella which he'd hung on the stand. 'But barking up the wrong tree, I'm afraid. I travelled on this train for financial reasons. You know how complicated train fares are – I get a headache trying to understand them – but my wife discovered that a combination of my senior citizen's railcard and the top off a packet of soap powder entitled me to a return fare of 50 pence on this train but not on any later ones. The train was full of elderly people smelling of soap powder. But anyway, I didn't have any choice, not with my wife clipping it off and presenting it to me.'

'It must be very difficult being so wealthy and famous, Kate,' Annabel sighed as they followed him out of the buffet, 'particularly if you're an artist and sensitive. There must be a temptation to play it down all the time so as to put ordinary people at their ease.'

'There's a darn in his left elbow,' observed Kate, watching him stagger slightly under the weight of the suitcase.

'Honestly, Kate! The lengths to which he'll go.'

'Doesn't it seem funny that he's carrying Connie Cauliflower around himself, Annabel? Wouldn't that be the publisher's job? What do publishers do exactly?'

'They get the authors' books printed. And take them out to expensive restaurants to cheer them up when they can't think of anything to write about. At least, I think that's what they do. I suppose it's up to him who carries Connie Cauliflower around.'

Annabel was abstracted again, turning over in her mind two very important subjects which she badly wanted to raise with T. P. Roseland but unable to decide whether she had the nerve.

There was little chance anyway while carrying Connie Cauliflower to a waiting bus and getting her aboard. She was, as her creator had said, light but awkward. With the half-hearted approval of the conductor – only Connie's smile won him over – they stood her on the platform where she took up most of the available space, leaving just sufficient room for the suitcase to be stood on end beside her if people were still to be able to squeeze past. She was, inevitably, the subject of much interest among other passengers. They sat down on the long sideways-facing seat just inside the bus, Annabel in the corner nearest to Connie, T. P. Roseland next to her in the middle and then Kate.

So squashed together were they, so intimately cosy as the bus moved off, that Annabel took the plunge and produced from her shoulder-bag her book of poems, this being the first of the two subjects she wanted to raise with him.

'I wonder,' she said, nervously, 'if you'd mind giving me your opinion of these. If it's no trouble, that is.'

Having handed the book to him, she looked quickly away with a somewhat faster beating heart for of course it is no light thing if you are, potentially at any rate, also an artist and sensitive, to expose yourself to criticism, particularly when the critic is a giant of English literature whose opinion can't easily be shrugged aside. Anyway, he might consider it a cheek to be asked.

Out of the corner of her eye, she saw that he had put his monocle to his eye and was turning the book over, studying its cover.

'Nicely produced,' he commented. 'Wish my publishers took as much care over my books.'

She then averted her gaze altogether, staring intently at the passing scenery while listening equally intently for the turning of pages (too fast would mean he was skipping some, too slow that he was thinking about something else) and any sounds of approval or otherwise.

The signs were encouraging. The page-turning rate seemed right and there were occasional little murmurs and grunts of apparent approval.

'I like this one particularly,' he said at last. 'It reminds me of home.' He began to murmur the poem out loud:

It's spring again, long winter's o'er
Peace at last from the vile bandsaw
Unstop one's ears. Phew! That is good
They've finished cutting firewood
But hark! A new sound takes the air
In field and pasture and fox's lair
A tractor's grinding round the edges
Yes, it's time to cut the hedges.

'I don't want to carp,' said T. P. Roseland, frowning a little, 'but I'm not quite sure about the reference to "fox's lair". It doesn't seem quite . . . quite appropriate.'

'It was really a practical question,' Annabel admitted. 'I couldn't find anything else to rhyme with "air". But I thought it sounded generally *evocative*.'

'Of course it does,' said T. P. Roseland, entirely satisfied. 'I'm being unimaginative. Anyway, I'm all for facing up to facts.'

And now that's done at last – oh lor'!
The tractor's roarin' off once more
But now, instead of roun' and roun'
It's charging crossways, up and down
Yes, it's farmhand Charlie
Ploughing, sowing wheat and barley.
Now May's in bloom and from above
Sounds which are not that of a dove
Roars from the ground, howls from the skies
An aircraft, spraying pestici . . . es

'I like that,' said T. P. Roseland, appreciatively. 'Pestici . . . es. I suppose you'd call that a sort of *elision*, would you? A rhyming elision.'

'I don't know if there's a technical term,' said Annabel. 'But it made things fit. I thought it justified.'

'Utterly,' agreed T. P. Roseland. 'More than that – innovative.'

> Glorious June, din every day
> They're cutting, turning, baling hay
> July, the combine's out till dark
> Drowning blackbird, chaffinch, lark
> The engine's stopped – oh, lovely! Fab!
> Just Radio One belting from the cab
> And now . . . ? No tractor, combine, saw –
> Yes, smoke and flames, they're burning straw
> Harvest, silage, hay's all finished
> Surely noise will be diminished
> Maybe now we'll hear a bird –
> Hark again! What's that I heard?
> A rumble, coming slowly closer
> Stop one's ears and hold one's noser
> We will get no peace today
> 'Tis the muck-spreader on its way
>
> It's autumn or – some say – the fall
> We hardly heard a bird at all . . .
> A screeching, screaming new refrain
> They're cutting winter wood again

The bus was already entering Addendon. The time had flown. T. P. Roseland sighed appreciatively and handed the book back.

'That's my kind of poetry. Better than most of the piffle I read. If I were a publisher I'd snap it up but unfortunately I'm not. Try my editor at Magpie Books, Linda-Jane Gaiters. She publishes a lot of poetry and she's coming to the Book Fair. She's bound to be at the wine and cheese party you were talking about, never misses anything like that. Pity you can't catch her there, parties put her in a good mood – the wine makes her excitable and daring. Though I can't guarantee her taste in poetry is the same as mine. Probably not, we don't agree about anything else.'

Annabel ignored the teasing which she'd come to expect. A feeling of euphoria, of supreme excitement and well-being, was creeping over her. This was an amazing day.

'Linda-Jane Gaiters. Remember that, won't you, Kate. Can I mention your name, Mr Roseland?'

'You can but it's probably not advisable. It could spoil the effects of the wine.' Annabel ignored that, too.

The euphoria was still with her as they got off the bus outside the Three Tuns and made their way with their respective burdens to the Black Dog, the smaller, cheaper and – so T. P. Roseland averred the moment he saw it – *cosier* establishment a little way along the High Street. They made an unusual spectacle in Addendon, Annabel and Kate in front with Connie Cauliflower smiling between them, T. P. Roseland grunting along behind with the suitcase, hat and tie askew, face flushed, umbrella under arm. Annabel felt it was a pity there was no one about to see them – they had even been the last to get off the bus – but that was too small a matter to interfere with her euphoria.

For this was a truly remarkable day. They had met T. P. Roseland, they had taken tea and sausage sandwiches with him and he liked her poems and had given her an introduction to Linda-Jane Gaiters. They might even be going to share the same publishers. It took time for such things to sink in but when they did . . .

It remained while he disappeared inside for a few minutes, emerging with Mr Burdon, the landlord, in tow to pronounce his satisfaction with the Black Dog and tell them that there was a room available for him and a cupboard for Connie and to thank them for their help and express the hope that he'd see more of them at the Book Fair.

True, there remained to be resolved the second very important matter she wanted to raise. She almost raised it now but her nerve failed her and instead she satisfied herself with asking if he'd need any help getting Connie to Willers in the morning. There was, after all, plenty of time for the other thing.

'We could come and give you a hand if you like. Couldn't we, Kate.'

'That would be *very* useful. It's a problem moving Connie around on my own by public transport. I used to have,' he said with a certain

39

wistfulness, 'two cars, both vintage, but for the moment I'm making do without any. If you really mean it, come round about ten in the morning. Incidentally, I don't know your names. My friends call me "Pip". Short for Philip.'

They left him carrying Connie Cauliflower inside, assisted by Mr Burdon. The landlord, not known as a sentimental man, was handling her tenderly.

'I told you there'd be a communion between us, didn't I, Kate,' Annabel said after a period of silence on the way home.

'I was just thinking. You still haven't got his autograph.'

'Plenty of time for that. There are more urgent things to think about at the moment.'

'Such as?'

'My poems, for one thing. How to catch Linda-Jane Gaiters at Mrs da Susa's wine and cheese party while she's feeling excitable and daring.'

'Don't be silly, Annabel. We can't get into the wine and cheese party.'

They had arrived at the corner of Badger's Close and they halted, prior to parting. Annabel turned her head to look at Kate and Kate saw that she was in an exalted, trance-like state.

'On a day such as this, Kate, a day upon which we have become friends with – in my opinion – the greatest author the world has ever seen after Shakespeare – no, why after Shakespeare? *He* never created a character as good as Connie Cauliflower – a day upon which he has praised my poems and invited us to call him "Pip", anything is possible.'

'You're not thinking of gate-crashing?'

'Today is a magical day, Kate. *Anything* is possible.'

'You're not allowed into the party, though, are you?' said Mrs Bunce vaguely when Annabel told her that she and Kate were going to Lord Willoughby's. 'It's just for these authors and artists and people, isn't it?'

'Today, Mum, is a magical day. Anything is possible.'

'Well, don't stay out late and don't make nuisances of yourselves.'

Mrs Bunce assumed that Annabel and Kate were merely going to hang around the school gawping at the distinguished visitors and collecting autographs. Such were not in fact Annabel's plans although exactly what they were she was herself far from sure. Perhaps T. P. – Pip – Roseland would be of help, for Annabel did not for one moment believe those jokes about not having been invited.

To be ready for any eventuality she had put on her brilliant yellow shirt, the tails hanging out over bright green trousers, and sleeveless orange jumper. A very dashing, literary sort of outfit, she felt. Her book of poems was in her shoulder-bag together with two spare copies, neatly printed out on pages cut from old exercise books and stapled together; also her autograph book.

But all she really knew was that this was a star-appointed day. Its magic must be given free rein to run its full course, hither and thither, wherever it might will.

Chapter 3

*****

Ostensibly, the wine and cheese party in the gym at Lord Willoughby's was simply a convivial gathering at which guests at the Book Fair were able to meet their hosts and the local *media* people in a relaxed, friendly atmosphere. The smooth hum of conversation and clink of glasses concealed, however, many fervent hopes and deep anxieties.

Mrs da Susa, for instance: what lay behind her attentive, appreciatively laughing exterior as, in best frilly white blouse, long blue skirt, and pearls, she chatted with Linda-Jane Gaiters, Jim Troops, Mollie Pike, Mr Toogood and Mr Ribbons?

First and foremost, an urgent desire to please. To have got these people to Addendon's first Book Fair was a triumph, but if unimpressed they would not come again and Mrs da Susa had dreams of this becoming an annual event, famous in the publishing calendar. She had conceived the Book Fair primarily, of course, from a desire to encourage reading and a love of books amongst her pupils and others. But there were secondary motives. It was, for instance, something that the headmaster, Mr Trimm, wasn't involved in, that she could lord it over free from interference. It was a heady experience which she wanted to repeat.

Still more excitingly, it was an opportunity to mix with literary people and flex once more those intellectual muscles which she had begun to fear might be atrophying. Mrs da Susa, too, was looking for soul-mates.

The idea of the Book Fair had come to her as she lay awake one night, kept from sleep by the contented snores, interspersed with little chuckles in his dreams, of Mr da Susa, and wondering if she were wasting herself in Addendon. Here she was, a graduate of two great universities, Oxford and London, stuck in a place where the level of thought seldom rose above the next jumble sale or who'd got planning permission on their garden. Sometimes it was only the remembrance that Lord Willoughby's needed her which kept her from walking out.

Where, oh where were those equal intellects, those whetstones against which she could sharpen the true steel of her own mind? Her husband's, alas, was not one of them, dear though he was – her ears were assaulted by a complicated triple snore with following gurgle – Salvatore was a darling but how many times had she looked up from some stimulating and controversial point in the *Observer* or *Times Educational Supplement* only for her comment to die on her lips as she looked at him.

Nor was Mr Trimm's. Clever enough in his own dull way, no doubt, but with a *closed mind*.

But today, perhaps, she had met the kindred spirits she yearned for, getting off the train at Querminster station. She didn't want to lose them.

And Linda-Jane Gaiters. What were her preoccupations as she sipped her white wine, left hand resting lightly upon upper right arm? Only her straying eyes betrayed the fact that her mind was not on the small talk but on the representatives of the local *media* – that is, the Addendon and Querminster papers and the radio stations, BBC and Independent, who were at the party. Yes, she was thinking of Jim Troops' new book.

'Are you sure it's a good place to launch a book?' the Chairman had asked her at the weekly editorial meeting. 'Where is Addendon?'

'I don't know exactly, Ted, but its location isn't important. Just keep your ears open and listen to the publicity coming from there from Friday onwards.'

'I'm off to the country for a few days to stay with my son and his family. My little granddaughter's seven and I value her opinion greatly. I'll ask her to keep her ears open too.'

'I'm sure, Ted, you'll get a positive response.'

Jim Troops' preoccupations were the same as Ms Gaiters' while Mr Ribbons, politely though he smiled behind his rimless glasses and attentively though he listened, was thinking about his manuscript: *All The Better to Eat You With – A study of medieval capitalist practices as exposed in folk tales: a discussion book for primary schools* and wondering how to raise the subject with Ms Gaiters. It had been rejected by Magpie Books some time ago, as indeed it had been rejected by every publisher he had sent it to, as had eleven other of his manuscripts. Possibly a face to face chat might resolve any difficulties. He had already given a copy to Maureen Marone when driving her from the station and she had promised to give him an opinion.

And then, of course, Annabel. Although not strictly speaking at the party she was very nearly so, hanging around outside with Kate and peering in through the windows. Her preoccupations we know.

Her immediate hope was to spot anyone who might be able to help her gain entry to the party and introduce her to, or at least point out, the people she ought to approach, in particular Linda-Jane Gaiters. T. P. Roseland was the likeliest candidate being both friendly and not, on his record, a stickler for protocol. If one thought about it, he was probably the only candidate. All she could see at the moment, however, was Mrs da Susa standing with a group of people.

'I'm always particularly keen,' Linda-Jane Gaiters was saying, 'on visiting schools because you teachers are so deeply involved in the reading experience. You are, I like to say, in the front line.'

'Or as I sometimes put it, in the trenches,' chuckled Mrs da Susa. She was enjoying herself more all the time despite her anxieties. 'But we do try here, at Lord Willoughby's, not to make literature that *austere legacy* of which *Harvey Darton* wrote.'

This statement was a great success and elicited a little murmur of approval, almost like a round of applause, from her listeners. She blushed, modestly.

'We don't need to concern ourselves too much with a *"writerly élite"*,' nodded Ms Gaiters.

'I hope, though,' Mollie Pike pounced in severely, 'that doesn't mean you let your kids read the sort of rubbishy stuff they've been conditioned to like through over-exploitative promotion. Stuff that doesn't stretch them.' There were further murmurs of approval and some head-nodding.

'Oh, we stretch them, don't we, Mr Toogood.' Mrs da Susa was jauntily confident after the success of her previous remark. 'We're stretching them all the time –'

She broke off, startled by the sight of a face pressed against a window and staring at her. The face immediately withdrew, leaving an impression on the window for a moment before this vanished, too. It had looked like Annabel Bunce of the Third Year but it must have been an illusion.

'It's my view,' Linda-Jane Gaiters was saying, 'that the kids should be directed to books from which shared meanings can be socially built rather than merely and idiosyncratically experienced.

'I think you'd be happy with our approach here,' laughed Mrs da Susa, adroitly sliding round that

47

one which was a bit deep, without notice, even for her. How thrilling this was, though! What a blast of fresh, keen, intellectual air these people brought with them! Balm to the soul of someone stuck in the thankless job of Deputy to Mr Trimm. (Where was Mr Trimm, anyway? He hadn't even bothered to come to the party. *Philistine!*)

What was that? The face at the window again – a different window – already melting away again like a Cheshire cat. It must be the wine. She must be careful not to have too much. It wouldn't do to become silly at her own Book Fair.

Linda-Jane Gaiters was taking her by the elbow, drawing her conspiratorially aside.

'Mrs da Susa, I wanted to warn you –' she glanced about her and lowered her voice still further ' – something rather dramatic is going to happen in the next few minutes. Something unexpected and perhaps a little alarming if you're not prepared for it.'

'You're expecting the unexpected?'

'A sensational – well, fairly sensational – occurrence. I thought I ought to warn you.'

'What about the others present? Won't they be startled?'

'That is the object,' Ms Gaiters explained patiently. 'I wish them to be startled, particularly the media people. It's for publicity.' She glanced about her again and her voice became scarcely audible. 'It's the opening of our campaign to publicize Jim's new book. A sensational book.

It'll revolutionize children's literature, the biggest breakthrough since *Alice in Wonderland*.'

'Not a case of over-exploitative promotion, I hope,' chuckled Mrs da Susa but the chuckle died away as she saw the expression on Ms Gaiters' face. It had been a joke in poor taste. Only over-excitement had caused her to make it.

'Can you give me a hint of what this occurrence will be?'

'I think you'll enjoy it more,' replied Ms Gaiters, 'if it's a surprise. You have only a few minutes to wait.'

She sauntered away, sipping her wine alertly.

'The only thing I ask of a book,' Jim Troops was saying in a loud, authoritative voice, 'is that it mustn't be *comfortable*. There've been too many *comfortable* books in the past. Say what you like about my books but they're not *comfortable*.' Mrs da Susa joined in the comfortable murmurs of agreement but her mind was now elsewhere, still thrilling to what Ms Gaiters had said. The biggest breakthrough in children's publishing since *Alice in Wonderland! To be launched at her Book Fair!* Even allowing for pardonable over-enthusiasm on the part of Ms Gaiters, her excitement was understandable. The Book Fair was almost an institution already.

She glanced about her, tensing herself pleasurably for the shock of the unexpected. From which direction would the sensation come? Through the door? Or a window? She noticed that one of the tall windows in the end wall of the gym was slightly ajar. Perhaps that ghostly face at the window had something to do with it. Or would one of the guests at the party do something sensational, or mildly so?

There was no hint of that, so far as she could see. All were conversing and munching and sipping quite normally. Linda-Jane Gaiters herself had stopped to listen, frowning, to Mr Ribbons whose beard was wagging conspiratorially close to her ear. Could Mr Ribbons be involved? Oh, surely not – wait, though! One person was behaving slightly suspiciously. Martin Mulloon, the author, was standing alone, looking lost, glass on the table beside him, hands clasped behind his back. He might be secretly holding something – *preparing to throw it*! Or was he simply feeling lost?

Mrs da Susa started as the door opened but it was only Maureen Marone returning. She had gone out a few minutes ago. She was now holding something in her hand as if not quite sure what to do with it. It looked like rolled up pages of an exercise book.

Another touch on her elbow made Mrs da Susa start again. This time it was Mollie Pike.

'Mrs da Susa, I was listening to your views about children's books with very great interest. You obviously have very firm and radical convictions about them and they happen to coincide rather closely with mine. It set me wondering if you'd care to do a little reviewing for the literary magazine I help to run. It has only a tiny circulation but we are very challenging and controversial and we flatter ourselves that it's quite influential among teachers and librarians. You might find it rewarding to have a vehicle for your views.'

Surely this would rank amongst the two or three most exciting days of Mrs da Susa's life!

'That would be the only reward, I'm afraid.' Ms Pike giggled deprecatingly. 'We can't afford to pay anything.'

Who cared about that? Only moments ago an outsider, now suddenly part of this thrilling literary world . . . Muriel da Susa, reviewer! Licensed to praise or sneer, to be quoted on dust jackets. Ahead, perhaps, promotion to the *Observer*, *Times Lit. Supp.*, discoursing learnedly on radio programmes . . .

'I'd be *delighted*.'

'Good. I'll sort out some books for you. In fact, I know what I'll do. To start with I'll give you –'

Ms Pike threw her wine in Mrs da Susa's face.

At least, so it seemed to Mrs da Susa during the fleeting moment of astonishment before she realized that the action had been involuntary; that Ms Pike had simply jerked her hand towards her mouth in order to stifle – unsuccessfully – a shriek, the glass just happening to be in that hand.

Blinking affronted through the wine, Mrs da Susa saw that Ms Pike was staring past her shoulder, an expression of frozen horror on her face. She was turning rapidly to see the cause of this when from behind her came a piercing yell, dwarfing Ms Pike's shriek as the Telecom Tower dwarfs Bloomsbury, followed immediately by the clang of a window bursting open – the same window which she had previously noticed to be ajar – then a pandemonium of further shrieks as guests recoiled and scattered before the struggling figures which came toppling into the gym as from the sky, just catching the edge of the table.

The table crashed over. Glass and crockery shattered and an avalanche of cheese, french bread, celery, cocktail onions and broken glass slid into a wine-drenched heap on the floor.

So startling was it, so complete the confusion, that for a moment it was unclear to Mrs da Susa how many struggling figures there were but as a camera flashed, revealing that at least one of the *media* people was alert, she realized that there were, in fact, no more than two people involved.

If, indeed, one of them was a person and not some terrifying invader from space. As they continued to writhe on the floor she glimpsed a monstrous, gleaming red dome of a helmet, black garments, glistening red boots.

The definite human being was Annabel Bunce.

Chapter 4

*****

After half an hour of peering through windows Annabel's confidence had begun to waver. It was evident that T. P. Roseland was not, after all, at the party. It was also getting cold.

'Perhaps,' Kate had suggested, cautiously, 'it's true he wasn't invited.'

'Don't be silly, Kate. If you think about it I suppose what he really meant, but was too tactful to say, was that he wouldn't be seen dead at Mrs da Susa's wine and cheese. Someone like him must be used to proper parties.'

'Anyway, I can't see any hope of meeting this editor. Let's go, Annabel. It's getting awfully cold.'

'Today, Kate, is a star-appointed day. Whatever happens will come suddenly, out of the blue.'

But Annabel spoke with less conviction than before. She had felt there was a momentum, that miraculous things would keep on happening, and was disappointed.

She cheered up a little after bumping into Maureen Marone while stepping back from a window. Ms Marone, who perspired easily in warm rooms, had been out for a breath of fresh air. Recognizing her as a distinguished visitor but not sure which, Annabel promptly apologized and proffered her autograph book and biro, squinting at the signature in order to identify her. Discovering that she had a well-known reviewer in her grasp, Annabel then produced from her bag one of the copies of *Collected Poems* (the book itself was reserved for Ms Gaiters). With a confidence born of T. P. Roseland's comments on them she asked if Ms Marone would be kind enough to read them and give her an opinion.

This Ms Marone promised to do, not having her wits sufficiently about her to think of an excuse. Having no bag with her (though she was wearing her hat) or pockets, she went sailing off back to the party with the rolled-up poems clutched first in one hand, then the other.

'That's something accomplished, anyway,' said Annabel. On any ordinary day the encounter would have been memorable but her expectations had risen.

'What about calling it a day, then?' Kate wheedled. 'After all, perhaps it's a magical week. Perhaps the magic's exhausted for today but there'll be more tomorrow.'

Thin though the argument was, Annabel seemed prepared to accept it.

'All right, Kate. Just one more look round, though.'

She went for a last saunter along the wall of the gym, glancing in at each window as she passed. She was still reluctant to leave, however, and instead of turning back when she reached the corner she hesitated for just a moment, then made to continue. There were two more windows to the gym round the corner, in the end wall overlooking the bicycle sheds at the back of the school. She hadn't so far looked through those.

Then she halted, staring at something. Putting a finger to her lips she beckoned Kate who joined her stealthily.

Standing on the ledge of the further of the two gym windows, back towards them and pressed into the frame was an extraordinary figure, a youth presumably but like none they had seen before in Addendon, hulking, brutish and menacing. Huge chested with monstrously high, wide shoulders that jutted arrogantly outwards and upwards and clad in garments of dingy fringed black leather. Black all over save for the huge, gleaming red dome of his crash helmet with little white wings on it and – most menacing of all, his boots: calf-length boots of glistening red with vicious great toe-caps. Across the back of his jacket some legend was printed in exploding red letters of which only the last three were visible – *OOT*.

This sinister lout, this epitome of all louts, this prince of hooligans, was peering furtively into the gym, oblivious to all else but the wine and cheese party. His intentions could only be evil. As they watched in amazement he moved, stealthily extending a black gloved hand towards the window which was already slightly ajar, pushing at it, tensing himself, about to spring.

Annabel sprang first, grabbing a leather-clad

arm as he launched himself in. Checked, he scrabbled to keep his balance then seized her wrist with his free hand to prevent himself falling backwards, dragging her with him. She put a knee on the window ledge to gain purchase and with *her* free hand grabbed *his* wrist and hauled back. Kate, gathering her wits, sprang to help but too late. He was toppling, pulling Annabel into the gym with him. She was forced to step up on to the ledge. Someone inside – Ms Pike – shrieked and Annabel answered with a spectacular yell as she felt herself going. Locked together they crashed inside, the window swinging open before them. The edge of a table broke their fall and then they were rolling on the floor together. Oblivious of the confusion and destruction around her, Annabel sought to pinion his arms to his sides. He was putting up little resistance, no doubt shaken by the fall, but he could still be capable of mischief. She needed help and Kate was still climbing in through the window.

Someone, quicker-witted than the others, was coming to give it . . . a lady in a dress of pale blue and grey alternating stripes. She was gripping his arms, holding him down . . .

No she wasn't. She was helping him to his feet, fussing over him, solicitous as a mother hen.

Annabel was left lying on the floor. So astounded was she that she made no move, just lay watching till a number of people including Kate, Mrs da Susa and Mrs Jesty, came to help her up, too.

56

But just as astounding was what followed. Having assured herself that Annabel was unhurt, Mrs da Susa looked at the lady in the striped dress and said, in a voice tremulous from shock and with perhaps something of an edge to it: 'So *this* is what you were expecting, Miss Gaiters!'

It wasn't the remark itself. That was merely baffling. It was the name.

So, after all, Annabel had come face to face with Linda-Jane Gaiters at the wine and cheese party: suddenly, out of the blue.

This day was truly living up to its promise. Truly, truly, a star-appointed day.

Linda-Jane Gaiters had been as disconcerted as anyone by these events – perhaps more so since it was her carefully planned publicity stunt which had fallen, literally, flat on its face. Her first priority was to get it back on its feet again. Having satisfied herself that the lout was unhurt she swiftly raised his hand on high.

'Ladies and gentlemen,' she cried to a still partly cowering audience, 'that was a spectacular introduction to a spectacular new hero, a hero for the twenty-first century. Twentieth century literature gave us Peter Pan, Toad, Bunter, Biggles, William, the Famous Five –'

'Connie Cauliflower,' muttered Annabel, bewildered but instinctively loyal.

'Yesterday's heroes, unreal, élitist. Today I give you a hero for the ordinary boy and girl, one who looks and talks and thinks like them but with

57

that teeny-weeny but exciting difference that he has magic powers. I give you –'

She twirled the lout round as if doing the Gay Gordons to reveal in full the exploding red-lettered legend on the back of his jacket.

SUPERBOOT

'– Superboot!' she cried in shrill confirmation. The lout raised his other arm and performed a little skip and dance.

While her audience digested this and cameras flashed Ms Gaiters, having put first things first, was able to turn her attention to Annabel and Mrs da Susa. It had already occurred to her that some profit might be derived from the fiasco. It had given her an idea for a slogan. She must build up to it carefully. She placed a hand on Annabel's shoulder.

'For this very brave girl,' she said, patting the shoulder with each word, 'we must all have the greatest admiration. What's your name, dear?'

'Annabel. Annabel Bunce.'

'Obviously Annabel saw what she believed to be an intruder and with great courage she tackled him. She wasn't to know that this was a carefully planned piece of publicity and that Superboot was intended to come flying in through the window on a rope positioned for that purpose.' Ms Gaiters' pats became heavier and more meaningful as she prepared to deliver her slogan. 'Yes, a *very* brave girl but I think she will have learned –' her voice became shrill '– that *it doesn't do to tangle with Superboot!*'

She kicked Superboot on the ankle while leaning over to murmur rapidly into Mrs da Susa's ear: 'Don't worry about the breakages. Magpie Books will pay.' And to a publicity assistant standing behind her: 'Nina, go and find a dustpan and brush.'

Taking the hint, meanwhile, Superboot leapt back on to the window ledge where he flexed his mighty shoulders before adopting a striking pose with hands outstretched above his head and crash helmet turned to one side. Cameras flashed again and there was applause, almost entirely from two sources. Mr Ribbons was clapping with slow and deliberate enthusiasm, hands extended straight in front of him. Ms Pike was pecking hers together quickly and a little dutifully as if she might have reservations. Perhaps she would have preferred *Superbootess*. Ms Gaiters smiled brilliantly.

Annabel was only just coming to terms with two remarkable thoughts: that this yob of deliberately menacing appearance, encountered skulking on a window ledge, was apparently to be applauded; and that the person she had wanted desperately to meet, who had the power to publish poems, was now patting her shoulder.

True, she was not so far very taken with Ms Gaiters. She did not really care for those patronizing pats, nor for the enthusiasm for the obnoxious Superboot. As for tangling, it seemed to her that

Superboot had learned that it didn't do to tangle with her, Annabel.

Still, no one was perfect and as publisher of Connie Cauliflower and friend of T. P. Roseland Ms Gaiters deserved respect.

Ms Gaiters was awaiting further reactions. The silence that followed the applause was broken by Len Higginson, photographer for the *Advertiser*.

'Looks like a yob to me,' he said, fingering his moustache. 'A big yob.'

Ms Gaiters smiled brilliantly again. She seemed pleased by the remark. 'We expect controversy, don't we, Jim, in fact we welcome it. We know that some people will hate Superboot but we don't care because Superboot speaks to the kids of today in a language they understand. No great breakthrough was ever made without controversy, was it, Jim, so the more people who don't like it the better as far as we're concerned. Controversy gets books talked about, especially on television. But I don't know why I'm telling you this. Jim is the genius who thought of it. Come on, Jim, and tell us all about it.'

Jim Troops came and stood modestly beside her, folding his arms so that the holes in his elbows showed.

'Superboot's a character the kids can identify with. Without his boots he's just an ordinary, typical, loud-mouthed, ignorant non-book-reading kid you can find hanging about on any street corner looking for something to vandalize. But by putting on these boots – I won't spoil it for you by revealin' how he gets 'em – he acquires magical powers and the moment he hears of over-oppressive authority anywhere in the world – it may be something perpetrated by some vicious right wing dictator in Central America or just some unscrupulous bent copper in Manchester – he puts 'em on and soars off, leaping across continents, maybe, and whoomph! puts the boot into the villain and rescues his victim.'

'Brilliant!' sighed Ms Gaiters. 'Thrilling action combined with a profound moral message. Kids always think they're being got at, too, and this will give them the feeling they're getting their own back. Jim is now available for interview. I'm giving the local media the chance to get in first because television will be here tomorrow.'

As a final flourish, Superboot demonstrated 'putting the boot in', lashing out with one foot and in the process losing his balance. He hurriedly jumped off the ledge and disappeared towards the bicycle sheds.

Uproar now broke out as the media besieged Jim Troops while other guests complained to each other about how Magpie Books were hogging all the publicity. There were bumps and bangs as the table was hoisted upright and the debris collected in bins by a team which included Nina, Mrs Jesty, Mr Toogood and Kate, who had been roped in because she was standing nearby. Supervising this was a shaken and brooding Mrs da Susa.

Cleaning up the mess after Ms Gaiters' misfiring publicity stunts was not what she had put on her best blouse and pearls for. She had looked upon Ms Gaiters as a kindred spirit and believed the feeling to be reciprocated but a kindred spirit would hardly have been so casual about ruining her wine and cheese party. It was all very well to say airily that Magpie Books would pay and carry on standing to one side and talking to Annabel Bunce. For Ms Gaiters it was just another party whereas for her, Mrs da Susa, it was to have been the high spot of the year.

If only Ms Gaiters had kept her properly informed of the publicity stunt this fiasco probably wouldn't have happened. She would have seen to that. And now she had gathered that television was coming next day. That was all very fine and desirable but it would have been nice to have been properly told. This was, after all, her Book Fair, not Ms Gaiters'. She skated briefly on some cocktail onions before they squashed. The wretched things had rolled everywhere.

Ms Gaiters, meanwhile, had kept her hand on Annabel's shoulder, apparently unwilling to let her go, as indeed she wasn't until she had made quite sure that Annabel was perfectly happy and there would be no complaints from parents.

'Now, Annabel, you're quite sure you're not hurt in any way? Clothes not torn?'

'I'm all right.' To have Linda-Jane entirely to herself was the dream situation that Annabel had vaguely imagined when coming to the party.

'I'm sorry you were misled by our little publicity stunt. I should like to make amends in some way –'

Now Ms Gaiters wanted to do something for her. It was all in keeping with the day. There was no problem there. Annabel reached into her bag which throughout her struggles had remained on her shoulder.

'I should like,' said Ms Gaiters, 'to give you a copy of Superboot signed by Jim –'

'No thanks,' said Annabel. 'I was hoping, though, that you'd look at my poems and see if they might be worth publishing. I've got them here.'

Ms Gaiters' expression became wary. Removing her hand from Annabel's shoulder she took the little book and fingered it doubtfully. Although Annabel didn't as yet sense it, the high water mark of the day had been reached. The tide was about to turn.

'I could look at them, certainly, though I can't promise anything, of course. Our poetry list is rather full just now.'

'I wouldn't want any favours. Only if you like them.'

Having nothing in which to carry the book, Ms Gaiters tucked it under her arm.

'Now you're sure you wouldn't care for a copy of Superboot? Perhaps you don't realize that this would be the very first signed copy in existence. Jim would put the date and time on for you and a special message –'

'No thanks –'

Ms Gaiters looked nettled.

'– but what I'd really like, if you've got it, is a new copy of a Connie Cauliflower book. I should like,' said Annabel, diffidently, 'to congratulate you on being the publisher of the Connie Cauliflower books. Isn't it a pity that Mr Roseland didn't come to the party?'

'Pip Roseland!' Ms Gaiters looked alarmed. 'Why should he have come? He's not in Addendon, is he?'

'Er – he's at the Black Dog.' Presumably Ms Gaiters was annoyed because she'd have liked him to come to the party and he hadn't bothered. He probably did this sort of thing quite often.

'He hasn't got that ghastly Connie Cauliflower with him, has he?'

'Er – yes. She's at the Black Dog as well.'

At this point the day's tide, having slopped about on the turn, began to ebb with gathering speed.

'Honestly!' Words began exploding from Ms Gaiters in all directions. 'That should have been thrown away years ago. What sort of image does it give of Magpie Books just when we've got our Superboot promotion going? At every book fair he follows me around with that Connie Cauliflower thing.'

'Why don't you buy him a new one, then?' asked Annabel, shocked but as yet unable to take in the enormity of what Ms Gaiters was saying.

'*New* one?' Apparently never in her life had Ms Gaiters heard such a disgusting proposal. 'It's easier to get rid of the wretched books which is precisely what I shall do. I shall pulp them.'

'Pulp?'

'Destroy the books we have in stock. Stop selling them!' Ms Gaiters became icy. 'Connie Cauliflower, as the Americans say, is last year's potatoes. Out. Fini. She can go on the compost heap. The modern world is no place for a cauliflower as a heroine, especially a well-spoken cauliflower in what appears to be a middle-class garden.'

'She's a perfectly ordinary cauliflower,' replied Annabel, also coldly. The last thing she wanted was to be unfriendly or rude to Ms Gaiters but there were limits to what she could be expected to take. 'And she doesn't own the garden, she's just a sort of worker in it. She's probably well-spoken because she read a lot when she was little. You want people to read a lot, don't you, so why insult them when they do?'

'Connie Cauliflower isn't even liberated. While Charlie Cucumber lies in bed she cleans the glass of his frame.'

'Would it be better if she were as lazy as him? And leave the glass dirty and get the nice gardener into trouble? What would you have done in her position?'

'Connie Cauliflower,' snapped Ms Gaiters, 'can go and get boiled. I am not in publishing to produce things like that. Not when we have brilliant authors like Jim Troops with books like Superboot.'

Annabel's lip began to tremble. She thought of her poems and of how the opportunity to meet a publisher, one who was well disposed towards her, even keen to do something for her, might never occur again.

She cast the thought out of her mind.

'I think Superboot's a creep,' she said. 'I love Connie Cauliflower.'

The tide had ebbed so far now that there wasn't anywhere much for it to go. Ms Gaiters decided that this was no place to lose her temper and, though still frosty, calmed down.

'Then I'm afraid you're not in tune with current trends. Perhaps you haven't been properly taught. I'll have a word with your teachers . . . Now, if you'll excuse me, Mr Troops has gone for a radio interview and I must see how he's getting along.'

'Did you mean it about pulping Connie Cauliflower?'

'Most certainly.'

She went off, transferring Annabel's book of poems to her other arm and almost bumping into Maureen Marone who was wandering around with her copy now tucked into her right sleeve. Kate had appeared at Annabel's elbow, the clearing up being finished.

'I heard some of that,' she said. 'T. P. Roseland wasn't teasing, then.'

'Oh, Kate, I thought Connie Cauliflower was for all time. I didn't realize they could just . . . pulp her. Finish her off.'

'But, Annabel, if you want Linda-Jane Gaiters

to look at your poems it's silly to quarrel with her. *And* after going to all that trouble to meet her!'

'My poems have to take second place, Kate. Let's go, shall we.'

On the way out, Annabel did dispose of the remaining copy of her poems to Mollie Pike whom she happened to hear talking about reviewing as they passed but, as she explained to Kate, it was only because she may as well. Her heart wasn't in it for the moment.

'If it's a choice between the world getting my poems and keeping Connie Cauliflower then it doesn't take long to choose, does it, Kate.'

'But is it a choice? It's not as if you can *do* anything about Connie Cauliflower, is it.'

'I don't know, Kate, I don't know. Let's find Mr Roseland. Oh, Kate, I thought this was a magical day, a star-appointed day. But it was only a great big bubble and now it's burst.'

Chapter 5

*****

'Well, I did say I'm not much in favour at Magpie,' said T. P. Roseland. 'Though I must say I hadn't realized quite how little. You're sure you didn't misunderstand her? She did say "pulp"?'

'Yes. Pulp.'

'So small a word but signifying so much. It has an aggressive, explosive quality about it, don't you think? You can't say it without spitting contemptuously. You don't suppose she was letting off steam a bit? She might think better of it when she's cooled down?'

'Perhaps,' said Annabel, without conviction.

'No, I don't think so, either. To be candid, it's no great surprise. It's kind of you to come and tell me, though. Look, they've got a garden here. Let me buy you a lemonade or something. To Connie's memory, perhaps.'

They were standing on the pavement outside the Black Dog, Mr Burdon having obligingly dug T. P. Roseland out of the bar after Annabel had insisted to Kate that they must find him immediately and tell him the situation.

'Of course it's our business,' she had retorted, when Kate had tentatively raised the question. 'It's the business of everybody who loves Connie

Cauliflower. The sooner we tell him, the sooner he might be able to do something about it.'

He didn't look as if he meant to as he brought the drinks out to a table, lemonades for them, a beer for himself. He had his monocle jammed into his eye for no apparent reason; perhaps, thought Kate, because holding it in gave him something to do with his face. It must be hurtful to hear that your books are going to be pulped, that they're finished, however brave a front you put on it.

Annabel was staring at him, coming to terms with her new image of him, reassessing the darn in his jacket, the dated suit, the cracked shoes.

'Faded gentility,' he commented with a smile, noting her interest. 'I'll try to make it a positive virtue in future instead of resisting it.'

'We thought you were a millionaire. Didn't we, Kate.'

'I was fairly comfortably off when Connie was selling well but things deteriorated after Linda-Jane became editor. She's never really liked Connie. She feels Connie isn't making enough meaningful statements about the times we live in, though I'm not sure I agree with her there, and that she isn't pushing back boundaries of various sorts. She's probably right about that because although Connie's had no great advantages in life she's remained a very sweet, good-natured, well-mannered cauliflower who doesn't like to hurt or offend anybody.

'Anyway, that's why I've had to hump Connie

round to book fairs myself to try to sell my books, and I can see that it's getting on Linda-Jane's nerves.'

They had the garden to themselves, sitting hunched against the cold. Kate's lemonade sent a chill through her but somehow it seemed right to feel bleak when Connie Cauliflower lay dying. She hadn't, of course, read the books herself but she liked T. P. Roseland very much.

'I could try another publisher, I suppose,' he said, 'but I expect they're all much the same. Looking on the bright side, my wife'll be pleased that I can stop going to book fairs.'

'But you can't just let her be pulped, Mr Roseland.' Annabel still hadn't had the courage to address him as "Pip". 'It's not fair to deprive the world of her.'

'It's nice of you to say that but I don't see that I can prevent it. Anyway, perhaps Linda-Jane's right. Connie's probably too gentle for a modern heroine. This Superboot character sounds more in keeping with the spirit of the times.'

'I think Superboot's a creep,' said Annabel, for the second time.'

'Ah, but you may be unusual. Perhaps we're both unusual. I don't know, do I. Mind you, I think Connie might have been all right if only they'd given her the sort of publicity they give to books they get excited about, like Superboot, for instance. If only Connie had had a few dumpbins and shelf-wobblers –'

'A few what?'

'Dumpbins are what they display books in, in shops, to make them catch the eye. And shelf wobblers go on shelves and wobble. I'm not entirely sure why but publicity people tell me they're good for bringing books to people's attention, though the best thing of all, of course, is television. If only Connie had had some of that sort of publicity!'

He sighed, polishing his monocle with his handkerchief.

'Dreams. I shall take Connie home and put her in her last resting place, probably the back porch. I think she'll fit in there and her smile will be a nice welcome for guests.'

'You'll let her make a last appearance at the Book Fair while she's here, won't you?'

'Not much point, is there. Anyway, there's nobody available to walk around in her. Linda-Jane's not going to allow any of her staff to do it when Connie's due for pulping anyway. She was reluctant enough before.'

Annabel fortified herself with a swig of lemonade then put to him the second of the two questions she had first wanted to ask on Querminster station.

They parted soon afterwards, T. P. Roseland to reenter the Black Dog, Annabel and Kate to walk home. Since his reply to her question, Annabel seemed revived.

'What were those things he mentioned?' she asked Kate. 'Dumpbins and . . .'

'Shelf-wobblers.'

'Shelf-wobblers,' repeated Annabel, and again: 'Shelf-wobblers.'

At 11 a.m. the following morning Mrs da Susa was hurrying along a corridor in Lord Willoughby's School, keeping well to one side to allow a rush of visitors to flow past and muttering and giggling to herself as was her habit when excited. The first Addendon Children's Book Fair had been in progress for an hour and she was starting to glory in it.

Visitors, children and adults, were crowding in at a most satisfying rate – busloads had come from Querminster and Cogginton – and the team from the children's television programme *Red Duster* had already arrived, earlier than expected, and were preparing to film Superboot. In the Assembly Hall, focal point of the Fair, publishers were selling their books and three authors, Sheila Carew-Singlesmith, Martin Mulloon and T. P. Roseland, were available for signings.

(The arrival of T. P. Roseland, whom she had forgotten about, had created some confusion. He had brought a caseful of his books with him and asked if he might have a table to sit at. However, Linda-Jane Gaiters, his publisher, had reacted quite violently when it had been placed – naturally enough, one would have thought – near the Magpie stand, saying there wasn't room for it there and it must be placed on the opposite side of the hall. T. P. Roseland had accepted this meekly but it was odd. There must be some difference of opinion between them.)

Other events were taking place in the classrooms. In one, for example, Mollie Pike was conducting a workshop for parents, teachers and librarians. In another, an artist wearing a frog's head was telling stories. In a third, Maureen Marone was giving poetry readings.

All was going splendidly, just like (a little self-deprecating giggle) a real book fair.

It will be seen that the resentments of the previous evening had faded from Mrs da Susa's mind; this despite the fact that this morning it was still Ms Gaiters who was marching around looking important, the role Mrs da Susa had expected to play instead of what she was actually doing, i.e. pursuing Ms Gaiters with telephone messages and running errands for her. Her mission at the moment, for example, was to go outside to the television van and hunt around it for Ms Gaiters' favourite pen which she thought she might have dropped there while welcoming the *Red Duster* team.

Despite the fact, too, that on the previous evening events had continued to be – to put it mildly – unrelaxing. After the wine and cheese party Mrs da Susa had been looking forward to going home with her guests, Ms Pike and Ms Marone, and preparing for them a delicious dinner over which they would linger, discussing literature and her future role in it as reviewer.

Unfortunately, Mollie Pike had wanted to

know why it was Mrs da Susa who, after a taxing day, was preparing the dinner while Mr da Susa, who had been happily unemployed for several years, continued to read the paper and study the racing form. She would have liked to help with the vegetables but it was against her principles while *he* sat around. Had he done anything all day? Didn't Mrs da Susa, of all people, realize she was letting other women down? Mr da Susa had retreated to the bedroom to read his paper because he couldn't concentrate for the noise coming from the kitchen and Mrs da Susa had suggested, helplessly, that Ms Pike go and discuss the matter rationally with him.

This Ms Pike went off determinedly to do, returning quivering after fifteen minutes to say that he was incorrigible (Mrs da Susa knew that) and that she was deeply sorry, but it was against her principles to eat a meal in such circumstances and she would have to go out to the Three Tuns. Ms Marone had by this time gone to bed early saying she didn't like upsets and in any case the wine and cheese had been enough.

The da Susas had had their meal alone, as usual, discussing racing. It had all been very distressing at the time, Mollie Pike being the last person Mrs da Susa wished to offend, but fortunately no permanent harm seemed to have been done. Ms Pike had calmed down and been quite conciliatory by the time she returned.

To revert to Ms Gaiters, there was also the question of Superboot. Mrs da Susa had at first been dubious. Did he, perhaps, glorify loutishness and violence? Also, his domination of the Book Fair was annoying other participants.

For this morning Superboot was everywhere. As a giant cardboard cut-out he stood outside the school, swinging a welcoming boot towards visitors. As a picture, he soared across one wall of the Assembly Hall, presumably Central America-bound on urgent business to do with a right wing dictator. On a smaller scale he sprang from posters, strutted on ballpoint pens, floated on balloons.

Superboot, to use a publishing term, was getting the hype, a frenzied publicity campaign.

Dubious no longer, however, her reservations now seemed small-minded. She was, after all, a beginner at this sort of thing. It was Ms Gaiters' experienced professionalism that was bringing press and television to her Book Fair and she ought to be grateful for it and tolerant of any occasional error. Her role now was to learn from that professionalism. She had already set aside her outdated prejudices against Superboot and intended asking Ms Pike if it might be her first book for review.

Hurrying along the corridor, Mrs da Susa was mentally writing her review. Of course she hadn't read the book yet but she already knew she'd love it . . .

'. . . a book that speaks to today's children about important issues in language they can understand . . . that will turn non-book-readers into readers

. . . I beseech every school to have at least one copy . . .'

And a fantasy was taking place in her mind, which she was living out in her mutterings and giggles. It concerned the group of youths and girls who often sat on the low wall outside the Memorial Hall in the evenings, eating fish and chips and indulging in noisy horseplay, pushing each other off the wall and shoving each other about. Non-book-readers, all of them; she knew that because they were all ex-pupils of Lord Willoughby's and if she had occasion to walk past them, which she avoided doing if possible, they would furtively flick chips after her and call out things like 'Wotchit, Ma' to show their independence.

She had never made any response, even when a chip had fallen inside the back of her blouse, giving rise to much mirth. (She had walked on with dignity till she had turned a corner and was able to remove it in the privacy of a shop doorway.) She felt towards them only sympathy and a sense of her own failure. They had never been awakened to life's potential, to a realization that the world has more to offer than horseplay outside the Memorial Hall.

Why? Because they had never discovered reading. In literature lay the key and perhaps the key to literature was Superboot.

In her fantasy, Mrs da Susa was walking past the Memorial Hall and a voice behind her was calling out, amid giggles, 'Wotchit, Ma'. She was pausing, turning, not in anger but with a dawning

smile, offering the youth . . . a copy of Superboot!
Watching his superior sneer as he took it; a book!
The sort of stuff you get in schools! The sneer
turning to a look of grudging interest, his attention caught by title and picture. Returning quietly
some time later to see him lying along the wall,
chin on fist, engrossed as he bestrode continents
with Superboot and put the boot in for principle;
his friends peering over his shoulder, eager for
their turn, recognizing in Superboot someone like
themselves, another non-book-reader.

Seeing them in subsequent days and weeks,
their appetite for literature whetted and growing,
lying on the wall immersed in Dickens, Dosto-
evsky, Plato . . . animatedly discussing their
merits . . . all thanks to Superboot.

Very well, a fantasy, but surely one with a grain
of truth. She must read Superboot aloud in class.

Lost in these daft though worthy thoughts, Mrs
da Susa turned a corner and was knocked backwards by a huge, smiling cauliflower trotting
towards her.

Inside the cauliflower was Annabel Bunce.

Annabel's immediate instinct was to apologize.
The collision had been entirely her fault. She had
been moving much too fast for a large cauliflower
in a busy corridor.

She checked the impulse, however. It was best
to speak as little as possible in case Mrs da Susa
recognized her voice.

She had donned the costume half an hour

earlier in the bicycle sheds helped by T. P. Roseland and Kate. This was, of course, what she had been longing to do since first learning of the model's purpose and what T. P. Roseland had agreed to on the previous evening; though more from a good-humoured readiness to please her than because he thought it would serve any useful purpose.

Annabel knew that his own preference would have been to pack up and go home but she didn't feel any guilt over persuading him not to because of the plan she had in mind. It was a plan to save Connie Cauliflower from being pulped; though she couldn't tell him about it in case he felt obliged to veto it. She had first thought of it when he'd talked about dumpbins and shelf-wobblers and television.

True, the plan still wasn't properly formed though she'd been thinking about it every waking moment for the last fifteen hours or so. It remained only a *grand strategy* and the need to decide upon *tactics* was now urgent.

The strategy was obvious. Connie Cauliflower needed publicity. Television was coming to the Book Fair today – Linda-Jane Gaiters had said so – and television offered the biggest publicity of all. Therefore, television must in some way (the *tactics*) be diverted from the worthless Superboot to the deserving Connie Cauliflower. Once people were reminded of her they would want to buy the books again and when the publishers saw this they would get behind her too and instead of pulping her give her all those dumpbins and shelf-wobblers.

A desperate plan, perhaps, but where there was a will there was a way and Connie Cauliflower, though lacking Superboot's shock value, had a powerful weapon in her armoury – her smile.

The power of that smile had become apparent again as soon as Annabel had begun to walk around the corridors, getting used to the costume before making her entry to the Assembly Hall. T. P. Roseland and Kate had already gone there, T. P. Roseland to sign books, Kate simply to look around.

Because of its size, the costume had to be steered rather carefully around corners and through doors, some doors being too narrow for it to pass through at all. Otherwise it was so well-designed, so light, the arm-holes and eye-holes so well placed, the interior harness so comfortable, that Annabel quickly came to feel it was part of her and to experience a strange and enchanting feeling; that of *being* Connie Cauliflower.

This arose from the reactions to her progress. Having prepared herself for mere interest and amusement, she got smiles. Slowly dawning smiles from children hanging on to the hands of parents, smiles from the parents, smiles even from fellow-pupils of Lord Willoughby's unaware of whom they were really smiling at. Richard White winked at her and Damian Price gave her a pat. The sweet innocence of Connie's smile outweighed the eccentricity of being a walking cauliflower.

Autograph books and scraps of paper appeared in her path. T. P. Roseland had told her to expect this and she signed them *Connie Cauliflower* with a flourish, not feeling that it was in any way misleading because with part of her mind she *was* Connie Cauliflower.

Surely, seen on television, that smile would win hearts everywhere. She *must* decide upon tactics! Television could arrive at any time, perhaps not till this afternoon but possibly this morning.

Kate was approaching, also smiling. Annabel hadn't yet told her of the plan. It was still too vague. She completed an autograph.

'Mr Roseland's wondering where you've got to,' Kate whispered into an eye-hole. 'He's been in the Hall half an hour.'

'Half an hour!' Annabel sounded exalted. 'It seems like two minutes. I'll come now.'

'Television's arrived,' added Kate, turning away. '*Red Duster*. They're in the Hall getting ready to film Superboot.'

The response was startling. Connie Cauli-flower (or Annabel, as even Kate had to remind herself) remained motionless for a moment, then burst into a sudden sprint. Perhaps realizing that a sprinting cauliflower is too much for a populated corridor she then slowed, but only to a still speedy trot.

Annabel had panicked. Her tactics weren't

thought out. What was she going to do? All she could think of was getting to the Assembly Hall as quickly as possible.

At the corner of the corridor, trotting purposefully, she knocked Mrs da Susa backwards. It was a fearful moment, a moment almost of despair.

But as Mrs da Susa recovered, she was smiling.

'I'm sorry,' she said. 'My fault entirely.'

She was prepared to apologize to a cauliflower, one clearly in the wrong, that had been committing that normally most frowned-upon offence, running in the corridor.

The apology calmed Annabel instantly. There was no limit to the power of that smile – none. All she had to do was present it in front of the cameras for as long as possible. Those were the tactics. No others were required.

Resisting the impulse to say 'that's all right, Mrs da Susa', Annabel gave a one-thumb-up salute in acknowledgement and pressed on at a more decorous but still rapid walk with Kate in puzzled though relieved pursuit. In the doorway of the Assembly Hall she paused momentarily to survey the Book Fair.

Two rows of publishers' stands lined a central aisle, the Magpie stand prominent in the right-hand row and dominated by a pyramid of Superboot books. Between stands on the left-hand side T. P. Roseland was to be glimpsed, monocle to eye signing an autograph book, his table in an obscure corner between wall and stage. Annabel noticed that the curtains to the stage were drawn across, something that normally happened only once or twice a year when the school play or some other entertainment was being performed.

By the refreshment bar, near the stage on the right hand side, some youths were knocking a Superboot balloon about to the annoyance of other people. Annabel recognized them as among those who often frequented the wall outside the Memorial Hall in the evenings. The central aisle was crowded and she herself was already attracting attention. A small girl with fluffy golden hair was staring at her open-mouthed.

All this she absorbed at a glance. What really concerned her was the television team, filming at the far end of the central aisle in front of the stage. A red-shirted television reporter was interviewing Jim Troops, Linda-Jane Gaiters beside him. There was no sign of Superboot other than his giant picture on the wall.

Annabel suddenly realized the significance of the drawn curtains. Something must be set up behind there ready for filming, some Superboot publicity stunt.

Anything she could do must be done now. Instantly. More autograph books were appearing. Hesitate and she would be swamped.

She moved on again. Instead of going down the central aisle, however, she abruptly changed direction and made her way along the right-hand wall, behind the publishers' stands, avoiding the crowd and minimizing the chances of being seen by Linda-Jane Gaiters who was, fortunately, concentrating on the interview.

A few children ran between stands to watch her, amongst them the fluffy-haired girl, still open-mouthed. Annabel lumbered on.

Fortunately the steps up to the stage were wide, but she had to pull the end of the curtain well back to get her bulk past. She revolved slowly through the opening, backing on to the stage.

This was watched in astonishment by Kate. From the opposite side of the Assembly Hall T. P. Roseland happened to look up and glimpsed her disappearing. He adjusted his monocle in disbelief. Linda-Jane Gaiters and Jim Troops carried on talking to the reporter, having seen nothing.

The curtain fell to behind her.

Chapter 6

***

It wasn't dark behind the curtains, as Annabel had instinctively assumed it would be, but brilliantly lit, ready for television. Her arrival was watched by three people.

In the centre of the stage sprawled a young man in dirty T-shirt and jeans. Standing threateningly over him, truncheon raised and obviously responsible for having knocked him down, was a uniformed figure. The uniform was vague but could be that of some police force. In fact, the uniformed figure represented oppressive and over-zealous authority anywhere as it crushed the aspirations of downtrodden youth. Ms Gaiters was very pleased with this symbolism which she thought would have great appeal.

At the back of the stage, on a platform at about head-height, reached by a step-ladder, crouched Superboot, arms outstretched like a great bat, ready to spring.

It was clear what was planned. At any moment the curtains would rise and the television cameras focus on the sufferings of the downtrodden youth. And then – Superboot to the rescue! Superboot soaring down to put the boot in, give Oppressive Authority his just desserts and save his victim.

The Oppressive Authoritarian and the Down-trodden Youth (in reality Magpie Books' Sales Director and Area Sales Representative respectively) looked at Connie Cauliflower out of the corners of their eyes. Having been roped into this at the last moment by Ms Gaiters they weren't sure whether the entry of a cauliflower into the proceedings was planned or not. There had been no mention of it but with Linda-Jane you never knew.

Of Superboot's thoughts there was no clue. Perched on his platform with the curtains due to rise he was, in any case, helpless – but the curtains were already parting; Annabel had arrived in the nick of time. The Book Fair was coming into view . . . the stands, the crowds, the television cameras shooting the scene on stage as it appeared to them. The Downtrodden Youth cowered, Oppressive Authority waved his truncheon, Superboot gathered himself . . .

Ms Gaiters, standing beside the television re-porter, her attention concentrated on the tableau immediately in front of her, became aware of a ripple of laughter from behind. In view of the dramatic nature of the tableau this was discon-certing and she looked about her for the reason.

Connie Cauliflower had emerged from the wings and was crossing the stage at a trot. Before Ms Gaiters could react further she was placing her bulk and her smile directly in front of Downtrod-den Youth and Oppressive Authority, obscuring the confrontation.

In a strange, low, throaty voice she spoke to the cameras.

'I am Connie Cauliflower. There are eight books about me by Mr T. P. Roseland and they are available at all good booksellers.'

Perhaps all of this information was true, perhaps it wasn't. Annabel did not much care. It was something to say, to attract attention. She was merely applying the first basic rule of the publicist and it was working. The television cameras cared only about her.

'Will that cauliflower get off stage!' shrieked Ms Gaiters, gathering her wits.

The downtrodden youth scrambled to his feet as if thinking of pushing Connie Cauliflower away.

'Please,' said Oppressive Authority, lowering his truncheon, 'we're busy.' He went round to where Annabel could see him. 'Hop it.' He looked half charmed by Connie's smile, unsure whether to laugh or be angry.

Then suddenly he cowered and Annabel turned herself about to see why. There had been a scuffle from above. Superboot was jumping off his platform.

Superboot had been poised to spring when Connie Cauliflower had appeared in front of him. He had checked himself, but the platform was small and he had remained off balance, unnoticed by anyone, teetering on the edge of it with arms waving till there had come a point when he had to jump anyway if he weren't to fall. The downtrodden youth was standing, unaware, directly in his path.

Annabel pushed the downtrodden youth violently on the arm. Taken by surprise he staggered and half fell, half jumped off the stage. His place was instantly filled by Superboot, also staggering wildly. Trying to keep his feet he cannoned into Oppressive Authority, knocking him over, then clutched at Connie Cauliflower for support. In self-defence, Annabel pushed at his huge shoulder. It gave way. One moment it was a shoulder, the next it had fallen down inside his jacket and this creature of towering, arrogant menace had become misshapen with one high shoulder, one low one and a hump half way down one side of his back.

The shoulder was padding. Obvious perhaps, but so realistic had been the impression of menace and power that it came now to Annabel as a revelation. Then it was only someone pretending! Just as she was pretending to be Connie Cauliflower! They were as make-believe as each other.

And . . . surely . . . she could smell something faintly – perfume!

Annabel grabbed at the zip of Superboot's jacket and pulled. He snatched at her hand but too late to stop her ripping it down to reveal that beneath his leather jacket he was wearing a pretty pink blouse and that in future it will be necessary to refer to Superboot as 'she', the 'he' and 'his' used previously having been incorrect.

Applause now broke out among the not inconsiderable audience and in the excitement a half-eaten custard tart was thrown from the direction of the refreshments counter, just missing Superboot. The thrower was one of the Memorial Hall youths. Mrs da Susa, returning with Ms Gaiters' pen, was in time to observe this and the descent of her Book Fair into farce.

Not to be outdone, another Memorial Hall youth threw a Superboot book snatched from the Magpie stand which whizzed past Ms Gaiters' ear and had to be dodged by Superboot herself. A third threw a rubber snake, given away by the publishers of the Sebastian Serpent books. Annabel saw it coming and, realizing what it was, caught it deftly and showed it briefly to Superboot who screamed and shrank away, shuddering, half-turning her back on Annabel and presenting the back of her neck and a tempting little gap between her helmet and the collar of her pretty pink blouse, now just glimpsable under the leather jacket. Annabel lumbered forward and stuffed the rubber snake down inside the back of the pretty pink blouse. Superboot screamed louder and, jerking, ripped off jacket and helmet revealing herself as tall, pretty young Nikki Watson of Magpie's Publicity Department. She fled through one of the doors at the back of the stage, still jerking and tugging at the back of her blouse.

Connie Cauliflower was left mistress of the field.

A wave of exhilaration and euphoria now swept

over Annabel as she turned to face the cameras again. She had made the most of her opportunity, improvising brilliantly and memorably. All this riveting action had taken place before a television audience. In homes up and down the country the name Connie Cauliflower would be on lips, the image of her smile unforgettably in minds . . .

It was short-lived. For the first time since her impulsive arrival on stage she was able to pause and take stock of the situation . . . of the fury on Ms Gaiters' face, the affronted horror on Mrs da Susa's, the bemused look on T. P. Roseland's, the watching, laughing crowd . . .

But it wasn't any of these that burst the bubble. It was Linda-Jane Gaiters' words to the grinning reporter.

'You won't be using that, obviously.'

'We'd like to. But no.'

She had been living in a dream. Of course she should have realized the cameras were only recording, that it wasn't going out live. She hadn't stopped to think. She had been too carried away, obsessed with her plan.

It had all been pointless. For nothing had she offended so many people . . . Linda-Jane Gaiters and Jim Troops by turning their promotion into a low farce, Mrs da Susa by turning her Book Fair into a ditto . . . no doubt T. P. Roseland by doing this without his permission and making everything still worse . . . Emotionally, Mr Roseland's displeasure was going to hurt the most but that of Mrs da Susa and Ms Gaiters might well have more practical consequences should they discover her identity.

She had had in her grasp a relationship with Ms Gaiters, a real live publisher of poetry. She had been more than willing to risk that relationship for the sake of Connie Cauliflower. But to have risked it for nothing . . .

The nearest exits were the doors at the back of the stage, through one of which Superboot had disappeared, but she wasn't sure they were wide enough and it would be disastrous to get jammed. She leapt clumsily off the stage and trotted up the central aisle between the stands towards the main doors of the Assembly Hall. No one tried to stop her. People stepped back to let her pass.

She trotted past the cameras and Ms Gaiters, past Mrs da Susa and the Memorial Hall youths. She dodged round the little fluffy-haired girl who stood straight in her path, gazing adoringly. She did not look towards T. P. Roseland.

Then she was out in the corridor, still trotting. She could hear someone following but she wasn't able to look round to see who it was so she increased her speed.

Visitors arriving at the Book Fair saw the huge, smiling cauliflower sprint out of the main doors of the school and laughed to each other and said what tremendous fun this Book Fair must be. They didn't hear the convulsive sobs coming from its interior. They didn't know that it was a hunted cauliflower, a cauliflower at bay, destined for the pulping machines, her sweet innocent smile no longer required.

It was Kate who had followed. She caught up with Annabel in the bicycle sheds where, looking like Humpty Dumpty, she was half-sitting on a rail for chaining bicycles to. It was strange and disturbing to hear the sobs coming from that smiling face.

Annabel was weeping not for herself but for Connie Cauliflower, swept aside by Superboot who – yes – did have feelings or, as Ms Gaiters would say, compassion; provided it were fashionable and preferably a long way off and a suitable excuse for putting the boot in.

The one thing which could possibly have in-creased Linda-Jane Gaiters' unhappiness after her second promotional fiasco within twenty-four hours would have been to see a man with a large face, a shock of greying hair and smoking a long, thin cigar approaching. This was, however, too remote a possibility to enter her mind.

Until, that is, she saw a man with a large face, a shock of greying hair and smoking a long, thin cigar approaching. Clinging adoringly to his hand was a small girl with fluffy blonde hair.

Ms Gaiters was at this time about to leave the Assembly Hall in search of Nikki, as Nina had already done. She was anxious to get the whole thing set up again quickly in case the television people had to leave soon but Nikki must be hiding in shame somewhere. The television team were having refreshments, chatting and laughing amongst themselves, probably about Magpie Books. Probably everybody was laughing about Magpie Books except Jim Troops who wasn't laughing about anything and had gone off in a huff saying they were a useless publisher, and Mrs da Susa, the organizer of this terrible Book Fair, who had disappeared hoping to find the person who had been inside the Connie Cauliflower outfit.

A waste of time in Ms Gaiters' view though Mrs da Susa was welcome to waste her time if she wanted. It was better than getting under Ms Gaiters' feet. She (Ms Gaiters) had thought Mrs da Susa to be a kindred spirit, but anyone who couldn't keep better control of a Book Fair wasn't anybody's kindred spirit. It was a madhouse and she (Ms Gaiters) had told her (Mrs da Susa) that if this Book Fair had a future she (Ms Gaiters again) had no intention of being any part of it. That was partly why she (Mrs da Susa) had gone off in such a state.

But anyway, it was obvious that T. P. Roseland had master-minded this attempt to hijack the Superboot publicity and it didn't much matter who was the pawn he'd hired to carry it out. She'd have a row with him as soon as the queue had gone from his table and enjoy telling him how his books were going to be pulped.

'Hallo, Linda-Jane,' said the chairman of Magpie Books, removing the long, thin cigar from his mouth. 'Surprised to see me?'

'I – I thought, Ted, that you were having a few days off.'

'You know what I found out? That Addendon's only twenty miles from where my son lives. He's on the other side of Querminster. This is Emma, my granddaughter.' He squeezed the little girl's hand affectionately. 'I thought there'd be some fun things for her to do here and I could look at the way television handles the Superboot promotion. When's that due?'

While Ms Gaiters was groping to answer this question Mr Reilly patted his granddaughter's hand and said: 'I gather somebody else has been getting some television publicity. Emma's been telling me about it, haven't you, Emma. She ran on ahead while I was parking the car.'

His granddaughter nodded. 'Connie Cauli-flower,' she said.

'You loved it, didn't you. Tell Auntie Linda-Jane what happened.'

Emma fixed her gaze on some object beyond Ms Gaiters' left hip. 'There was a nice policeman and he was trying to arrest a horrible-looking criminal and the criminal wouldn't let him and Connie Cauliflower came to help the policeman and she was ever so brave and knocked the criminal over but he had a friend standing on a wall. The friend –' Emma shuddered '– was even more horrible than he was, he looked like the man who stole your car, Grandpa, and he jumped off the wall and was going to kick the policeman but Connie Cauliflower chased him away. She was very brave and clever, Grandpa. She put a snake down his back. She was,' added Emma, 'funny as well.'

Mr Reilly patted her hand again. 'Yes, that must have been very funny,' he chuckled.

'And, Grandpa,' continued Emma, 'the most horrible one turned out to be a lady in disguise.' She directed her gaze further away from Ms Gaiters and lowered her voice, disapprovingly. 'When she ran away she started taking her clothes off.'

'She's mad about this Connie Cauliflower character,' said Mr Reilly. 'Why don't we have books like that on our list?'

'It is on our list,' said Ms Gaiters, desolate.

'Oh, it's our publicity, is it? Good. Well done, Linda-Jane. I'm always telling people I've got the shrewdest operator in children's books working for me. Who's the author? Is he here?'

'T. P. Roseland. He's just behind you.'

T. P. Roseland had risen to his feet, having dealt with the queue. He was now anxious to find Annabel, also to escape from the Assembly Hall and Linda-Jane Gaiters. He surveyed guardedly the large hand thrust in front of him before taking it.

'Ted Reilly, Magpie Books. I don't think we've met before, Mr Roseland.'

'No, I don't think we have. Not when you were aware of my presence, anyway.'

'Marvellous books of yours. I hear our little bit of publicity went well. My granddaughter's very

taken with your Connie Cauliflower character, aren't you, Emma. Have you had a proper
promotion for your books recently?'

'Not recently, no. Or ever, I don't think.'

'Our present plan,' said Ms Gaiters rapidly, 'is
to devote our resources to Superboot. After that,
perhaps –'

'Grandpa, I don't like Superboot,' said Emma.
'That's who I was telling you about, the one who
looked like the man who stole your car. He's
Connie Cauliflower's enemy.'

'We'll give you dumpbins, posters, window
stickers, a promotional tour –'

'Shelf-wobblers?'

'Of course. When someone's as important to
the company as you are you can have anything
you like. Look, if you're not doing anything why
don't we find somewhere to have coffee together.
Emma would be thrilled, wouldn't you, Emma?'

'There's something I ought to attend to first . . .
a reader of mine who's been very helpful. I'd like
to thank her and perhaps arrange a little treat. If
you can give me a few minutes . . .'

'Give you anything you like. I'm glad I brought
Emma here or I wouldn't have known you were
with Magpie. Crazy business, publishing, isn't it.
I've been in it thirty years but I'm still learning.'

'Yes, it is,' T. P. Roseland agreed and went off in
search of Annabel. Fortunately he knew to look in
the bicycle sheds so he found her before Mrs da
Susa.

*

'I think your poems are hauntingly beautiful,' said Maureen Marone. 'Hauntingly, hauntingly beautiful.' She pressed the pages of exercise book into Annabel's hand.

It was later that afternoon and for Annabel only one more thing was needed to make perfect this deliriously successful Book Fair of Mrs da Susa's. Since this morning she had seen wonderful things happen, above all T. P. Roseland being interviewed for *Red Duster* with Linda-Jane Gaiters and Connie Cauliflower in attendance. (This time with Nikki Watson inside. Annabel had had a little jealous pang but it couldn't be helped for, alas!, her own brief appearance in the role must remain secret.)

As Connie Cauliflower's profile had been raised, Superboot's had been discreetly lowered. He had made no more personal appearances, perhaps for fear of ridicule, and although the posters, pens and balloons remained, the giant cut-out and picture had been removed, put away for another day.

Also, T. P. Roseland had informed Annabel, Ms Gaiters had promised to have Connie's glue renewed.

T. P. Roseland's table had been moved to a prominent position by the Magpie stand. He was seated there now, signing non-stop, keeping up a cheerful flow of chatter to book-buyers and autograph-seekers.

There remained Annabel's poems. And here,

from Ms Marone, was another marvellously encouraging verdict.

'Though just a little political for my taste,' added Ms Marone as she turned away.

'What did that mean, Kate?' The second statement had flawed the perfection of the first.

'I don't know, Annabel.'

Ms Marone had gone over to Mr Ribbons who was having a cup of tea at the refreshment bar. She was handing him a folder with what could have been a manuscript inside, saying something to him. He, too, looked first pleased then puzzled.

'Oh, well,' said Annabel, 'the main thing is she likes them.'

'I don't wish to be unkind,' said Mollie Pike, shortly afterwards, 'but I don't think your poems would have much relevance for today's kids.'

'They've got relevance for me,' said Annabel, 'or I wouldn't have written them.'

'Today's young teenagers are into pop, fashion . . .'

'We can think about other things, too. From time to time.'

'Of course, there are the bigger issues like inner city alienation . . . Look, for the attitude of today's kids to poetry I suggest you look at number 37 of my magazine, an article by Jon Whipple. I'll send a copy to the school library. Now, if you'll excuse me . . .'

'Two in favour, one against. You can't hope to

please everybody, can you, Kate. It's very promising. But Linda-Jane Gaiters is the big one.'

'I'm afraid,' said Ms Gaiters, 'that your poems would not sit easily on our list.'

'Does that mean you don't want them?'

'Yes, it does,' said Ms Gaiters, her composure slipping. She had had enough of this ghastly Book Fair. It had upset the whole power structure at Magpie Books, previously so cosily satisfactory. Ted Reilly and T. P. Roseland had had coffee together with Emma and then, after T. P. Roseland's television interview, lunch as well and had come back chuckling together like old cronies, positive *soul-mates* and talking about vintage cars and other boring things with which she couldn't compete. She knew Ted had an old Bentley or something. Apparently Mr and Mrs Roseland had been invited to the Reillys' home to see the thing.

It wasn't merely aggravating, it was worrying. If T. P. Roseland, now in favour, were to start complaining about her – unfairly, of course, but some of these authors would stop at nothing to get their books publicized – then, well . . . jobs weren't two a penny in publishing at the moment.

She'd have to adapt. Please Emma. Connie Cauliflower probably wasn't a bad series. She'd take a fresh look at it. Ease off Superboot just for the moment. She could string Jim along somehow. He'd gone home in a sulk but he'd see reason.

Although it didn't much matter who'd been inside Connie Cauliflower during that television fiasco she had a suspicion that this girl standing innocently in front of her talking about poetry could tell her a thing or two . . .

She recovered herself. It was undignified to lose her temper.

'Perhaps,' she said, summoning up some graciousness, 'you'd like to try again in a few years' time.'

'Thank you,' said Annabel, 'but I wouldn't want my poems to sit on a list where they're not comfortable. Perhaps,' she added, also graciously, 'I'll try another publisher's list, one with a broader base.'

'You don't look too worried about it,' said Kate, afterwards, when they were having drinks through straws at the refreshment counter and watching T. P. Roseland industriously signing. There was a look of well-being about Annabel.

'She suspects I was Connie Cauliflower, doesn't she, Kate. It might just be colouring her judgement.'

There was a long, very long, contented gurgle through the straw.

'I was willing to sacrifice my poems for Connie Cauliflower, Kate. If that's what's happened, so be it. I'm not going to start complaining now.'

Chapter 7

*****

It was the following morning and Mrs da Susa was driving distinguished visitors – such as had not already left for various reasons – to Querminster station.

'I don't believe I've read your books, Mr Mulloon,' she said, making conversation to the author beside her. There was a burst of noise from the engine as she absent-mindedly pressed harder on the accelerator instead of braking as she approached Querminster's first traffic lights. Luckily she had already absent-mindedly declutched with the other foot.

Concentrating wasn't easy when the first Addendon Children's Book Fair had just finished and you knew that it had almost certainly been the last and the dream of it becoming an institution had been nothing more than a dream.

Linda-Jane Gaiters had departed on the previous evening with Nikki and Nina, leaving the sales people to wind up the Magpie stand and repeating her view of the Addendon Book Fair. Jim Troops had already gone. Other publishers had left by car grumbling that they hadn't had a look-in for Magpie and there were plenty of decently run Book Fairs without bothering with Addendon's. Maureen Marone had left on the previous evening, too, in distressing circumstances which were now much on Mrs da Susa's mind.

It was all so unfair. None of it had been Mrs da Susa's fault but everybody seemed to be blaming her. Was there still something to be salvaged from the wreckage . . . the reviewing? It was all she had to cling to now.

'Probably not,' replied Mr Mulloon when the noise and jerking had died away and the car was at rest in the inside lane. He was, of course, referring to Mrs da Susa's remark about his books. He had a nasal, mournful voice. 'Not many people have.'

There was a jolly laugh from behind as Sheila Carew-Singlesmith showed her teeth. Beside her, in the rear seat, Mollie Pike was staring frozenly out of the window.

'They're about . . .' Mrs da Susa dredged her memory '. . . teenage romances. You reveal the dilemmas of young girls growing up.'

'You've been reading the blurbs. I was flattered by that. To think that after thousands of years of civilization it's been left to me, Martin Mulloon, to reveal these dilemmas. Not that anybody cares. My books sell about 1400 copies each. Only 1400 people interested in learning at long last about the dilemmas of young girls growing up.

'Actually, I haven't a clue about the dilemmas of young girls growing up and if I had I wouldn't be so ungallant as to reveal them. It's publisher's waffle.'

Mrs da Susa didn't want to hear this downbeat, cynical stuff. Her mind was on Mollie Pike.

There had been a full-scale row at home last night. Ms Pike had exploded over who should lay the table for dinner, saying that Mr da Susa, who was working on his stamp collection, could at least do that. She had gone off for another confrontation, returning after ten minutes screaming that he was a master of grinning obfuscation who would drive a saint mad. Mrs da Susa knew this and had laid the table. Ms Pike returned cutlery and mats to the drawers saying she would rather go without dinner than bend and she couldn't understand why Mrs da Susa didn't feel the same, not apparently realizing that she was asking Mrs da Susa to starve to death.

Maureen Marone, who still didn't like upsets, had meanwhile left almost unnoticed in a mini-cab with her luggage. Mollie Pike had subsequently gone to the Three Tuns again, leaving the da Susas to another meal alone. She had returned later but had since spoken only when essential.

So where did that leave Mrs da Susa's future as a reviewer?

Ms Pike suddenly spoke.

'So this is Querminster!'

The statement was greeted by Mrs da Susa with an enormous inward sigh of relief. It was clearly placatory, meant to restore good relations.

'A pleasant enough town, don't you think?' she replied buoyantly.

'I've seen worse.'

Not the mind-stretching talk for which Mrs da Susa still yearned but good to hear, nevertheless. She began to frame a cautious question about reviewing.

'Oh, look!' said Sheila Carew-Singlesmith, suddenly. 'There's Connie Cauliflower. We can't escape her, can we?'

Mrs da Susa glanced round. An estate car had drawn up beside them. It was the Magpie sales director's and in the back of it Connie Cauliflower lay smiling at them. The smile was so warm and so unexpected that it drove everything else out of Mrs da Susa's mind. A weakness came over her and she smiled back and waggled her fingers.

'One must admit,' she sighed, basking dreamily in the relief of resuming good relations with Mollie Pike and the chance to talk about literature, 'that there is something quite *uplifting* about that smile. Perhaps it's because it's so simple and innocent and pure. Don't you find it fills you with little yearnings, a feeling of what a rich and wonderful place the world is if only we could see it? Such positive feelings instead of dilemmas and ugliness and putting boots in ... I suppose it's silly to think that a cauliflower might have a point to make.

'I wonder, too,' continued Mrs da Susa, leaning comfortably back in her seat, one idle thought leading to another, 'if perhaps we make too much of books necessarily being a good thing in themselves. Perhaps they're only as good as the words inside.'

It was only little flights of fancy, a momentary lapse. She'd have pulled herself together given the chance . . .

I'm surprised,' said Ms Pike, 'to hear such naive romanticism coming from you, Mrs da Susa. Surprised and, I must admit, shocked that you of all people so misunderstand the purpose of literature.'

'I was merely speculating,' protested Mrs da Susa but, glancing round, she saw that Ms Pike was gazing frozenly out of the window again.

Hoots from behind announced that the lights had changed. The estate car moved away. In deep misery, Mrs da Susa tried to follow suit and stalled the engine. Hoots became blares and a stream of traffic passed on her right as she vainly tried to start it again while Sheila Carew-Singlesmith offered a hysterical chortle in the back. Glancing up in despair, Mrs da Susa was suddenly delivered of a strange vision.

A chauffeur-driven Rolls-Royce was gliding past, the sunlight sparkling in the depths of its glossy black paintwork. Through its rear window she saw, or thought she saw, a laughing face in the act of biting an apple. It was the same face she had imagined she'd seen through the gym window, thirty-six hours ago.

The face of Annabel Bunce of 3 G.

*

'I hope you're enjoying this little trip,' said T. P. Roseland, who was sitting between Annabel and Kate in the back of the Rolls. 'My philosophy, from long experience, is to make the most of every little pleasure because it will probably soon be snatched away.'

Annabel assured him that from their short experience they had come to the same conclusion.

The Rolls was Mr Reilly's. He had sent it over because he felt that an author of T. P. Roseland's stature ought to have suitable transport to the station. T. P. Roseland had offered Annabel and Kate a ride to see him off.

Their main treat as rewards for Annabel's performance as Connie Cauliflower was to be a visit to his home during the next school holidays to see his garden, the vegetable and flower beds where Connie and her friends had been born and brought up. Annabel had specially asked for that.

'I'll look forward to your visit.' T. P. Roseland, monocle to eye, face half-distorted, was searching his wallet for his 50-pence return ticket. 'You deserve a lot more than that, though. Connie's in with a chance again.'

'Connie Cauliflower,' said Annabel confidently, 'will live forever.'

'Perhaps, perhaps not. She's getting another print run, publicity. After that it depends on whether the books keep on selling. Linda-Jane will come fighting back with Superboot and other things. I've got you and Emma on my side but there are plenty of Linda-Janes on the other.'

'Oh, look, Mr Roseland – there's Connie.'

They were stopping at more traffic lights. To their right, in the outside lane, the Magpie sales director's car was waiting to turn off along the inner ring road, London-bound. Connie was smiling at them from the back.

'Off to London to get her glue renewed,' said T. P. Roseland, fondly. 'She must be very excited. Let's give her a little wave.'

'I know she'll live forever, Mr Roseland,' Annabel insisted. (She probably never would call him 'Pip', though she did now have his autograph.) 'Do you know why?'

'Why?'

'Because of the way everybody smiles back. Look at Kate now.'

'Anyway,' Annabel added after a pause, 'that's what I want to believe.'

The lights turned to green and Connie Cauliflower went smiling off along the inner ring road.

Annabel, Reaching for the Stars

*****

Chapter 1

*****

It was towards the end of dinner break that Kate began receiving reports that Annabel was standing on one leg beside the tennis courts. Vicky Pearce was the first to bring the news.

'I don't know what she's doing, Kate. She's refusing to say anything, just standing there with one foot in the air and arms spread out. Like Eros but without the bow and arrow.'

'On one leg!' Kate frowned. Then she remembered. 'It's April the first. Try somebody else, Vicky.'

'I'd forgotten it was April Fools' Day. Still, if you don't believe me, you don't believe me. Please yourself. I'm going to have another look and see if she's moved. There's quite a crowd gathered.'

Kate smiled in superior fashion and let her go. It was true that she had been wondering where Annabel had got to, but she wasn't going to fall for a feeble trick like that. Most likely Annabel and Vicky were in this together. Annabel would be watching her from some vantage point right now, waiting to shout 'April Fool'. Kate began putting the lid on her lunch-box.

She was sitting on her and Annabel's favourite bench in the school grounds. They had arranged to meet there to eat their packed lunches as usual but Annabel hadn't turned up.

This was surprising because Annabel was normally very reliable about appointments, but Kate had assumed that she must have been kept talking by Mrs Jesty, their history teacher. For some inexplicable reason Annabel had gone off to seek out Mrs Jesty and have a word with her about her *previous* term's report which was the reason she hadn't come straight out with Kate. But that had been nearly an hour ago. They couldn't *still* be talking. Anyway, what had there been to talk about in the first place? Perhaps nothing. Perhaps it had merely been a part of the April Fool build-up. Possibly some very elaborate joke was in preparation. Annabel didn't do things by halves.

Though Annabel hadn't seemed in the mood for jokes; had, indeed, been rather withdrawn for the last day or two. Kate had noticed it first on Saturday afternoon when they'd been doing some shopping in the High Street. She'd wondered if it had anything to do with Annabel's Auntie Lucy Loxby who'd been staying with the Bunces for the weekend but it seemed unlikely. Annabel was very fond of her aunt. That last term's report, then? It would have had to be a very *delayed* reaction. Anyway, what was supposed to be wrong with the report? Annabel hadn't complained about it at the time.

But where was Annabel now?

Richard White and Damian Price was ambling by, heading in the direction of the tennis courts.

'What are you sitting there for?' called Richard White. 'I'd have thought you'd want to be with your friend at a time like this.'

'Why?' asked Kate.

'Haven't you heard?' said Damian Price. 'She's standing on one leg beside the tennis courts.'

They went on their way, leaving Kate feeling uncomfortable. Was everyone ganging up to make an April Fool of her? Or were Richard and Damian merely victims? She looked at her watch. Soon be time for afternoon school, anyway. Perhaps she ought to be going indoors. Instead she put her lunch-box on her lap, folded her arms and stayed there just a little while longer.

A minute later, Fiona Turnbull arrived, breathless.

'Annabel's asking to see you, Kate,' she said. 'She's standing on one leg beside the tennis courts.'

As Kate continued to sit, perplexed:

'Come on, Kate. I think it's something urgent.'

Kate folded her arms more tightly and looked stubborn.

'Oh, well, I can't make you, can I. I'm going back. I don't want to miss anything.'

When she'd gone, Kate looked furtively about her. There didn't *seem* to be anyone watching. Rising, she hurried towards the tennis courts, moving more cautiously as she neared the beech hedge which concealed them from view. No one sprang out from behind it, however, and as she reached the opening in it she was able to see that there was indeed a crowd, quite a large one, gathered by the tennis courts. The attention of this crowd, which Fiona was now rejoining, was focused upon something unseen in the middle of it.

Or *appeared* to be. How elaborate was this hoax?

Setting caution aside, Kate walked boldly forwards and joined the crowd. Peering between heads she saw Annabel. She was standing on one leg, her left, with arms extended gracefully, just like Eros without the bow and arrow. Her left ankle, which was taking the strain, was quivering a little and her face was set but she looked calm. Near her, on the grass, lay her empty lunch-box, lid beside it. She must have eaten the contents while standing on one leg then thrown them down.

'Annabel!' Kate cried.

Annabel's eyes moved.

'Thank goodness you've come, Kate. Let Kate through, everybody. I want to talk to her. Privately.'

The spectators parted obediently but as soon as Kate was through they pressed round again trying to overhear.

'Please stand back,' Annabel cried impatiently, but since no one took any notice she cupped her hands round her mouth and whispered into Kate's ear, wobbling slightly.

'Kate, I'm sorry I kept you waiting but I know you'll understand when I explain. I want you to do something for me *very* quickly. I want you to go to the library and find the Guinness Book of Records and see if there's a record for standing on one leg and if so what it is.'

'You – you mean you're trying to set up a record? Is that what you're doing?'

'Quickly, Kate. It'll be first bell any minute. If there is a record I want to know if I'm close to breaking it. Because if I am it'll be worth staying here a bit longer and getting a detention for missing some of first lesson. I've already been here for –' Annabel squinted at her watch '– eleven minutes and it's all been in front of witnesses.'

'You're trying to set up a record, then –' Kate was still trying to grasp the situation. 'You're hoping to get into the Guinness Book of Records?'

'Yes, Kate, but please stop saying it. I don't want everybody overhearing and jeering if I don't. Especially Julia Channing. Her neck's getting longer every second. And please hurry, Kate. It's urgent.'

The first bell was ringing as Kate dashed into school and fled up the stairs to the library.

Reference section: Chambers Dictionary, Who's Who, Great Railway Locomotives of the World, Decline and Fall of the – the things I do for Annabel! – Fossils of the Lyme Regis Area – *Guinness Book of Records*! Hah! Now what's it under? Arts and Entertainments? Don't be silly! Human Achievements? Stretching things a bit but maybe ... North Pole Conquest ... Lunar

Conquest . . . nothing about standing on one leg
. . . *Miscellaneous Endeavours* – Ah! Apple-
peeling . . . bed-making . . . this is more like it.
Getting warm, surely, getting *very* warm. *Standing*! Still nothing about standing on one leg,
though. Maybe there isn't such a record. Maybe
the field's clear for Annabel to set one. Quick
check back, though. What's this? *Balancing on
one foot*! Note current record time, thrust book
back on shelf and flee as second bell shrills to
arrive panting and choking back at the tennis
courts. Crowd a little smaller now but not much,
people clearly reluctant to miss anything.

'Well?' whispered Annabel. The strain was beginning to show. She was concentrating hard,
swaying. 'Is there a record?'

'Yes.'

'What do I have to beat?'

'Thirty-two hours.'

Annabel's eyes flicked to her wrist.

'Just over twenty-two minutes, Kate.'

'Thirty-one hours, thirty-eight minutes to go.'

Annabel's disappointment was plain but there
was no hesitation. She lowered her foot.

'It was worth a try but I wasn't properly prepared. Come on, Kate, no point in being late for
lessons.'

She picked up her lunch-box and set off briskly
for the school, bewildered spectators opening a
path for her. As soon as she was clear of them, she
broke into a trot.

'They'll be late if they don't get a move on,' she

said, glancing back. 'As a matter of interest, Kate, who does hold the record?'

Kate, at her shoulder, was marvelling at how well her legs were functioning after their ordeal.

'Someone from Sri Lanka. A Mr Anandan.'

'Must have very strong legs, Kate. Sri Lanka, though, did you say? Could be something to do with eastern mysticism. Maybe he was able to go into a trance and sleep on one leg. We westerners can't really compete with that sort of thing. Wrong sort of record for us to try, probably.'

'Annabel, you didn't mention you were going to make an attempt on a world record. What made you –?'

But Annabel's legs had suddenly foundered beneath her and she had to cling to Kate for support.

Kate helped her indoors.

'I'm sorry I kept you waiting, Kate,' Annabel said again over hot chocolate in the dining hall during afternoon break. 'I thought I'd only be a minute or two with Mrs Jesty but one thing led to another. I was as surprised as you are to find myself' – she lowered her voice – 'attacking a world record, but there was a certain *inevitability* about it too if you know what I mean.'

Kate knew that Annabel was being evasive. She wasn't meeting Kate's eye but gazing fixedly over the top of her mug as she sipped to where Naomi Peach and Fiona Turnbull and other Third Years were deep in conversation round another table, perhaps speculating on what Annabel had been

doing at dinner break. Annabel still hadn't enlightened anybody except Kate and she hadn't
enlightened her very much.

'But, anyway, you saw Mrs Jesty,' said Kate,
patiently probing, 'though I'm still not clear what
about –'

'About last term's history report, I did tell you
that, Kate. But I'm afraid all that did was leave me
more dissatisfied than ever and then I met Mr
Birkett in the corridor and had a word with
him.'

'About last term's art report?'

'About careers. You may have forgotten, Kate,
that he's careers master as well as art. I think it
had slipped his mind too because he seemed quite
surprised to be reminded but anyway he took me
to the careers room.'

The careers room at Lord Willoughby's was a
cubicle, originally a large walk-in cupboard,
equipped with two chairs, some posters on the
walls and a collection of pamphlets.

'Careers!'

'I think he was pleased that someone was showing an interest. It was quite difficult getting away
once he'd started but I'm afraid I didn't find it any
more satisfactory than Mrs Jesty.'

The bell was shrilling. Kate finished off her hot
chocolate and sat back in her chair.

'I'm not following this, Annabel. For reasons
you haven't explained you discussed last term's
report with Mrs Jesty, then possible careers with
Mr Birkett. You then went outside and stood on

one leg. There doesn't seem any *logic* to your movements.'

'It's entirely logical, Kate. The sequence of events has a *ruthless* inevitability.'

Annabel reflected for a moment, then continued, cautiously:

'You see, I was in a very low state when I left Mr Birkett and I wanted to think things over for a few minutes before meeting you so I went for a little walk round the tennis courts first and I was feeling that the only answer was to *break out*, Kate, start thinking big, do something really *dramatic*. And then suddenly it came to me –'

'The answer to what, though, Annabel –'

'– set a new world record for something like the ones they have in the Guinness Book of Records. Pushing a bathtub, *anything*, but preferably something individual if that doesn't sound too selfish. And I wanted to try something right away and I thought of the record for standing on one leg –'

'Balancing on one foot is the official term.'

'Balancing on one foot then, and I couldn't wait to see how difficult it was so I lifted up a leg and there I was. In business! And the minutes went by and I ate my packed lunch and a crowd gathered and it seemed a pity to waste what I'd already done because for all I knew I might be on my way to a record at first go. But I didn't want to say anything to anybody because I could see Julia Channing all ready to scoff and sneer if she found out what I was doing and I failed. And Naomi

Peach was standing there looking superior. Did you notice her, Kate?'

'Naomi? She's all right. I thought you liked Naomi.'

'I've gone off her, Kate. All that charm's just hollow. Hollow. But, anyway, that's when I asked Vicky to find you.'

'Annabel, you still haven't told me. The answer to what?'

Annabel looked deep into her chocolate. It must be cold by now.

'To why I'm a nonentity. I want to make my mark in life, Kate.'

The dining hall was empty.

'I'll explain properly tonight, Kate. My thoughts'll be more organized by then. If you really want to know.'

'I do,' said Kate.

Chapter 2

*****

That evening, seated stiffly on the chair in her bedroom, Annabel began her explanation; the Great Explanation as Kate had come to think of it, such was the air of momentousness that surrounded it.

Kate, who was herself sitting on the bed, noticed that while speaking Annabel was frequently casting sidelong glances at her own reflection in the mirror, apparently appraising slight changes of expression, her favourite one being a narrow-eyed, sultry look to which she returned several times though without much satisfaction. She seemed to be doing this quite unconsciously.

'I suppose,' began Annabel, 'that it was Auntie Lucy Loxby that started it. She asked me what I wanted to do when I grow up.'

(Auntie Lucy Loxby had to be given her full name to distinguish her from Annabel's other Auntie Lucy, Auntie Lucy Lowe. Auntie Lucy Loxby was her father's sister, married to Uncle Leslie Loxby and Auntie Lucy Lowe was her mother's sister-in-law.)

'People are always asking me that,' said Kate. 'I never know.'

'I try to look sullen and uninteresting and hope

they'll think about something else. But do you know what she told me? That Mozart wrote his first sonatas when he was half my age. It pulls you up short, doesn't it, Kate.'

'Oh, Annabel! Mozart was a genius.'

'And I'm not. All right, Kate.'

Kate sighed.

'And – I don't know, Kate –' Annabel pouted her lips and studied the effect in the mirror '– it made me start looking at myself and wondering what I was doing with my life and what I'm going to do, if anything. Have you wondered about that, Kate? Not that *you've* any need to worry. I know you're going to be a successful human being. But have you wondered?'

'Successful at what?'

'Anything. Just being alive. Anyway, it made me get out my last term's report and look at it –' Annabel reached for the dressing table. 'Here it is, Kate. Tell me what sort of person gets a report like that.'

Kate studied the report which Annabel thrust into her hands. It looked the usual sort of thing. Better than usual, in fact. Not unimpressive.

Annabelle's (that was how she had to spell her name for French) *accent is good. If only she could make use of her undoubted abilities she could shine in this subject.* Not much wrong with that!

Annabel shows flair but does not always put in the required effort. You couldn't complain about that from Mr Toogood for English, especially when you *hadn't* put in the required effort.

It has been a thoughtful term for Annabel was Mrs Jesty's contribution for history.

'What's that mean?' asked Kate.

'That's what I went to ask her today but she didn't seem to know. She just seemed surprised to be asked.'

'I expect she was.'

Kate noticed that Annabel was now fingering her face as she stared at its reflection. She looked dejected. Kate turned to the summings-up. That of Mr Trimm, the Headmaster, was: *A reasonable term's work but Annabel must pull her socks up and make more effort;* of Mrs Jesty, who appeared again as form teacher: *We are still waiting for Annabel to fulfil the potential which we are all confident is there. We must all of us, teachers and parents, work together to achieve the results we are hoping for and know are possible.* No mention of a role for Annabel in this joint enterprise.

Kate handed it back.

'Honestly, Annabel! And you came eighth. What's wrong with that?'

'It's the report of a nobody, Kate, a nonentity. I think I'd rather be dramatically bad at everything than just . . . *nothing.*'

Kate sighed again.

'What about Mr Birkett? What did you talk to him about?'

'It was spur of the moment, Kate. I met him in the corridor and asked him what sort of careers might be open to me and he said had I considered engineering because they were very keen to have more girls and it's such a fascinating life. He was so enthusiastic I asked him why he hadn't taken it up himself and what it was anyway and he didn't seem too sure about that but anyway he cooled off when he found out about my maths. Then he asked me what ideas I had and I said I'd like to be a manageress of a sweet shop when I leave school.

'It was only a little joke, Kate, but he started looking up courses in trainee management and what qualifications I'd need. I didn't, of course, tell him what I'd really like to be, I never tell anyone but you, Kate, because it might sound conceited. But I had just thought that when I made my little joke about the sweet shop he'd laugh and shake his head and say that I wasn't setting my sights high enough because he'd been noticing me and I was obviously destined for very great things. That was partly why I made it . . .

'But you can't, can you, Kate, tell people that you'd like to become poet laureate or a great violinist or Minister of Agriculture.

'And then, Kate, he tried to see what else he could suggest and he looked through the papers and said there were sometimes very good clerical jobs going at Beldews for school-leavers but I'd have to brush up my maths.'

'Beldews on the industrial estate? Where Dad works?'

'Yes, Kate. It was after that I went and stood on one leg. Is the logic clear now?'

'Clearer.'

Annabel was staring openly at her reflection

now, twisting her face and wrinkling her nose as if taking pleasure in making herself look ugly. Her voice was suddenly high pitched.

'My spots look bad today, Kate. It's awful being boring and talentless and spotty and ugly. Breaking a record's the only hope I've got of achieving anything. I'll go through the Guinness Book of Records tomorrow and find one that's possible.'

'Record-breaking can't be as easy as all that, Annabel.' It was all Kate could think of to say. 'People all over the world have a go at them.'

'There must be something among the silly ones, Kate. Anyway, when you're desperate you have to try.'

Kate got up to go. Her mother would be expecting her home. At the front door she paused.

'Why do you want to be Minister of Agriculture, Annabel?'

'I've got a plan to encourage farmers to let more wild flowers grow and replace all the hedges and ponds and let their hens run free range and all sorts of other things.' Annabel was speaking more calmly now. 'Oh – and go back to horses. Horses are much nicer than tractors. My plan also solves all those over-production and unemployment problems and makes everything just perfect in every way. It involves payments to farmers on the one hand and bringing back the stocks on the other.'

'It sounds like going back to where we were before they invented machines.'

'Yes, it does rather, doesn't it. As you can see,

Kate, I should be a very *radical* Minister of Agriculture.'

At the gate, Kate was halted by a sudden cry.

'Of course it won't be easy, Kate, but I have to try. Is it so wrong to reach for the stars?'

Walking home, Kate decided that most of the Great Explanation sounded nonsense. Annabel had ne~ : bothered about her future before, had always proclaimed the virtue of positively not doing so. 'Just do what interests you, Kate,' she had always confidently said, 'and everything will work out.'

So what was making her desperate now? Did she know herself? Or was it something vague, some indefinable yearning, perhaps some sudden panic about herself?

At home, Kate looked out the previous Friday's *Advertiser*. On the front page was a large picture of Naomi Peach preening herself in Corton Compton village hall and flourishing a pen with which she was pretending to sign a contract. She was dressed in one of her bizarre outfits assembled from jumble sales and the Querminster Oxfam shop. This one made her look like a nineteenth century fireman.

Behind her, four grinning boys were striking extravagant attitudes as they strummed guitars or bashed drums. These were *Their Lordships*, a group who had first teamed up at Lord Willoughby's of which they had all been pupils. They played at local functions and some of the Lord Willoughby's girls had recently formed a fan club of which Naomi was secretary. Other members included Julia Channing, straining to get into the picture by peeping round the drummer's head, and Tracey Cooke.

The caption read:

> Naomi Peach of Lord Willoughby's School makes her first booking, for Corton Compton Village Hall, on behalf of *Their Lordships*. Attractive Naomi, of Marchmont Crescent, Addendon, is secretary of *Their Lordships* fan club and seldom misses a performance, and in gratitude for all her hard work they've invited her to become their honorary bookings secretary too. You can bet Naomi is thrilled and so are the rest of the fan club.

Was it coincidence that Annabel's urge to make her mark so closely followed Naomi's leap to fame? True, there had been no immediate signs of jealousy. On the contrary, Annabel had gone round showing the picture to people and laughing, saying *Their Lordships* would regret unloading their chores on to Naomi after they'd found themselves in the wrong village hall a few times and, anyway, Naomi wouldn't last long as secretary now. That 'attractive' would be too much for the others to bear. She'd be stabbed in the back in a *putsch*.

Possibly a reaction had set in though for Annabel wasn't laughing now and it was hard to believe that it was because of Auntie Lucy Loxby's innocent question about what she wanted to do when she grew up, still less the activities of Mozart. Annabel had herself said that she was 'off' Naomi.

Come to think of it, it had been after speaking to Naomi in the High Street that Annabel had first become withdrawn on Saturday afternoon. Naomi had got off the bus from Querminster carrying a large bag and Annabel had left Kate to go over to her and find out what she'd been buying, returning after a few moments muttering that it was a new outfit. But, yes, she'd remained silent and preoccupied after that, had seemed quite shaken, in fact, now that Kate analysed it . . .

Oh, but this was all imagination; hindsight. Annabel had probably been dreaming about a new outfit of her own or wondering what was for tea. Such thoughts were unworthy. When Annabel was reaching for the stars was it fair to grub around in the gutter for motives in this way?

After all that, Annabel's choice of record was something of a let-down. She announced it to Kate during break next morning after going through the Guinness Book of Records while seated together at the table in the school library.

'Onion-peeling!' Kate was surprised. 'That doesn't sound very glamorous. I'd have expected you to go for something . . . well . . . glamorous.'

'Nothing's glamorous in itself, Kate, only the achievement.' Annabel sounded nettled. She'd looked a little disconcerted when going through the records. Perhaps she'd expected them to be easier. 'I suppose *you'd* say marathon running isn't glamorous, just a lot of sweating and grunting.

'*I've* got to be practical, Kate. The only records I stand a chance with are the silly ones and I don't suppose any of them are what *you'd* call glamorous. I'm keeping bubblegum-blowing and cucumber-slicing as second strings but I expect you'd say *they're* not glamorous either, and having tried bubblegum-blowing quite often in the past I think the onion-peeling sounds easier though nothing's easy, of course, or it wouldn't be a world record.'

Kate made soothing noises.

'Sorry if I sounded touchy, Kate, but I don't stand a chance with the serious records, do I, though I could make a last check.'

Annabel flicked through the book again, starting from the back. She wasted little time on *Sports, Games and Pastimes* beyond pointing to a picture of a muscular Russian lady pounding along a track and saying, 'Wouldn't stand much chance against her, for instance, would I, Kate,' but lingered over the *Plant Kingdom* section which she found particularly interesting.

'There's a record for the longest daisy chain in the world, Kate. Nearly a mile long. Still, you need a team of sixteen for that and I don't want to get involved with teams. No, I've made my decision.'

She turned back to onion-peeling.

'50 pounds or 22.67 kilos of onions to be peeled and the present record is 5 minutes 23 seconds. And there has to be a minimum of 50 onions. So that you can't breed giant ones and make it too easy, I suppose.'

'Can you afford all those onions?'

'I don't suppose so, but where there's a will there's a way, Kate.' Annabel rose and put the book back on the shelf. 'The main thing now is speed. I'll try the onion-peeling tomorrow and if that's no good try something else on the following day. I want to become a world record holder by the end of this week. In fact I'd really like to have it in Friday's *Advertiser* if at all possible.'

The time for caution and secrecy was over. On the way downstairs Annabel was planning what to put on her sponsorship form for it would be mean, she said, not to use the occasion to help charity. She had five favourite charities amongst whom any proceeds could be divided. Also it would be best to keep one's options open and aolt to be sponsored for 'onion-peeling or any other record deemed appropriate at the record-breaker's discretion'.

'It's exciting, isn't it, Kate.' If Annabel had been disappointed by the choice of records open to her she was now shrugging that off. 'Just a few unpeeled onions standing in the way of immortality.'

She announced her intentions to the rest of the class at the beginning of dinner break when she produced her sponsorship forms in the classroom.

Made out on pages of exercise book, they also carried a request for a pledge of at least one large onion, to be brought to school next day.

The immediate consequences were jokes about her choice of record and an outbreak of record-breaking mania. Richard White, Damian Price, Fiona Turnbull, Edward Chance and Jason Fradley all shot off to the library to try to be the first to have a look at the Guinness Book of Records before dinner.

No one seemed to take Annabel's attempt very seriously.

'Personally,' jeered Julia Channing when declining to sponsor her, 'I would rather be known for *not* holding the world's onion-peeling record. I've never heard of such a silly, smelly-sounding record.' She continued to jeer at all record attempts and Annabel's in particular.

The derision only stiffened Annabel's resolve. She was committed now anyway. 'Say what you like,' she said to Kate, 'but it's a *practical* record. Let's see what the others come up with.'

She was concerned by the possible competition though and certainly, when you're trying to make your mark, it doesn't help to be one of a crowd, especially when they *might* come up with more exciting records than yours.

Still, the quest for sponsorships, resumed on the playing fields with Kate's help after they'd had their packed lunches, drew a generous response; perhaps because everyone assumed their money was safe, though it helped, too, to be first in the field. Many people seemed keen to bring an onion.

Back in the classroom at the end of dinner break other intending record-breakers were returning from the library with their plans. Fiona's were the most clearly thought out. She was, she announced, going to form a team to attack the record for the *longest daisy chain in the world*. She was also interested in the *longest conga in the world*, suggesting that if Addendon, Cogginton, Corton Compton and the surrounding villages could be induced to take part a conga of ten thousand might be possible.

Annabel, now clearly worried, told Kate that such plans were 'grandiose' and 'impractical'.

At four o'clock Annabel, with Kate in support, took her sponsorship forms to the school gates to catch people on their way home, only to find herself part of a throng of other intending record-breakers waving forms; a *clamour* of record-breakers, as she said dismally to Kate. They included not only Third Years like Fiona and Richard White but people from other years too. The craze was spreading. Annabel's attempt was becoming swamped.

There was, Kate observed, a poignant moment which afterwards she pretended not to have seen. Annabel, clamouring with the rest of the sponsorship-seekers, suddenly fell silent and started moving along the drive towards the school. Looking for the reason, Kate saw that Andrew Torrance of the Fifth Year was approaching, deep in conversation with another

Fifth Year boy. Kate knew that Andrew Torrance occupied a special place in Annabel's thoughts though one, alas, that he knew nothing about. Talented beyond his years at sport – especially cricket – and music and much else he looked, Kate thought, particularly dashing today, head bent, thumb hooked under the shoulder strap of his bag, smiling at something the other boy was saying.

Annabel presumably thought so, too. She was getting to him before anyone else could, paper and pencil held out invitingly, smiling winsomely – in a slightly sideways manner so that the less spotty side of her face was towards him – exercising her charm.

'Excuse me,' she was presumably saying, 'but would you care to sponsor my attempt on the world's onion-peeling record?'

Or perhaps she was suddenly overwhelmed by the thought of actually speaking to him. Possibly the topic of onions was freezing. It may be that Julia's words came back to her. But, anyway, he didn't notice her. He walked straight past.

Straight into the path of a wheedling, confidently chattering Fiona Turnbull. He was stopping, smiling, chatting, signing. So was his friend.

Annabel and Kate went home after that, Annabel speaking only once on the way. She said: 'I'm stuck with onion-peeling now, aren't I, Kate.'

The attempt was planned for the following day. If anyone cared.

*

There was a strong smell of onions in Assembly next morning and Mr Trimm sniffed wonderingly a few times. Some sixty members of his audience were carrying at least one large onion in their pockets, often several (many of them bruised after being tossed about on the way to school). That part of Annabel's plan, at any rate, had been successful. They were handed over to her at intervals during the morning and stored in her and Kate's lockers and desks in bags brought for the purpose. The aroma lingered all day.

The attempt was to take place straight after school in the kitchen of Annabel's home, Mrs Bunce having raised no objection. Vicky Pearce had agreed to join Kate as a witness for, as Annabel said: 'I'll need witnesses, Kate. Obviously I can't expect the Guinness Book of Records people just to take my word for it.' Kate had offered to take photographs, too.

All this was discussed in the classroom between lessons and at one point Kate noticed that Julia Channing, seated two desks away, was listening with interest. Kate thought nothing of it at the time.

Meanwhile Fiona Turnbull announced that her team for the *longest daisy chain in the world* had been recruited and work would begin on the school playing fields during dinner break, an ideal venue because of the ample space and plentiful supply of daisies.

At dinner break Annabel and Kate went to inspect progress and found Fiona working on a section of the daisy chain while at the same time attempting to supervise the work of her team who were engaged on other sections. It included Tracey Cooke and Miles Noggins but also a large number of First and Second Years, some of whom didn't appear to be taking their work very seriously. A number of spectators were drifting about.

Annabel started counting.

'You've got too many in your team, Fiona. There are supposed to be no more than sixteen. You've got at least twenty-five.'

'I can't help it. People keep joining in and doing bits.'

'Well, I'm sorry, Fiona. It's no use. The attempt's invalid. You'll have to start again and keep to the rules.'

'Oh, go and peel your onions,' said Fiona, rudely.

'My onions will be peeled under properly controlled conditions,' snapped Annabel.

They were distracted by shouts and laughter. Some Fourth Years, led by Big Mark Bailey, had snatched up sections of daisy chain and were running off with them, streaming them out behind. Fiona dashed in pursuit, yelling threats.

'I told you it was too grandiose, didn't I, Kate,' said Annabel. 'I don't think Fiona has the necessary organizational skills.' She seemed comforted.

At four o'clock, accompanied by Kate and Vicky and all carrying bags of onions, Annabel set off home for her own record-breaking attempt. Nobody remembered to wish her good luck.

At the Church Lane pillar box another record attempt was taking place. Richard White and Damian Price were trying to shove a number of First Years on top before leaping up themselves but all kept ending in a confusion of sliding bodies and yells of laughter. Annabel, Kate and Vicky gave it a wide berth.

'That's the sort of thing that gives record-breaking a bad name,' Annabel said disapprovingly. Perhaps, though, it helped give onion-peeling a quiet dignity.

At home, Annabel's mother vacated the kitchen saying, 'Hope your record attempt goes well, Annabel; *world* record, did you say? We *shall* be famous, shan't we,' and disappeared into the garden to do some weeding. Vicky Pearce, who was taking her role very seriously, ostentatiously laid her watch on the draining board and then checked the kitchen scales with some weights she produced from her pockets, pronouncing them accurate.

Annabel, much impressed by these preliminaries, put on her apron, selected her knife and prepared to weigh out the onions. Now that the time for action had arrived she had set all reservations aside and was geared up for action.

She was, she said, 'going for gold'.

Chapter 3

It would be pointless to give a detailed account of why Annabel Bunce of Badger's Close, Addendon is not today the holder of the world's onion-peeling record, an honour still held at the time of going to press by a Mr Alphonso of Pennsylvania, USA: enough to mention some of the unexpected problems.

The onions, large though they were, proved when weighed to be not nearly large enough, amazingly providing nowhere near the required weight. Fortunately Mrs Bunce, called in from the garden, was able to make up the difference from her own stock but Annabel was unnerved by the resulting pile.

Some of the onions were very strong and many difficult to peel. Worst of all, Vicky Pearce proved unexpectedly officious.

'I can't pass that onion,' she said, after an already weeping Annabel had thrust her first one aside. 'It's not properly peeled. There are bits of brown on it.' After some hasty further work she was still unsatisfied. 'I'm sorry, Annabel. I can still see brown bits. Look.'

Annabel started slicing the brown bits off.

'I'm sorry, Annabel, this is a peeling, not a

chopping record. I am going to disallow that onion.'

They were all crying by now. When Kate, wiping her eyes, produced her camera, Annabel jerked her distorted face away. 'I don't want my picture taken,' she sobbed. 'You were right about it not being glamorous, Kate. Whoever's got it's welcome to it.' She seemed on the point of giving up but then soldiered on.

After 5 minutes 23 seconds, the record time, she had peeled 24 onions with a total weight of some 11 pounds – 5 kilos – and was red-eyed and hysterical. Vicky Pearce left in a sulk with her weights saying she wouldn't be a witness for Annabel again in a hurry and Annabel went upstairs to think things over. Perhaps her heart hadn't really been in it, anyway. Perhaps, deep down, she had known it to be a mistake.

Kate left soon afterwards with a carrier bag full of onions presented to her by Mrs Bunce. She made onion soup for the family that evening.

Annabel was unusually quiet on the way to school next morning but she didn't seem as upset as Kate had thought she might be. She apologized for what she described as 'the mess'.

'I should have listened to you, Kate. You weren't very keen on onion-peeling and you were right. You always are.'

Julia Channing was loitering by the school gates. She fell into step along the drive.

'Did you break the record?' she asked.

'I don't see that it's of any interest to you but since you ask, no. It wasn't a proper attempt, anyway, just a sort of trial run for the real thing.'

'That's all right, then. You won't care that it wouldn't have counted.'

'Why not?'

'You didn't have proper evidence. You've got to have independent adult witnesses and newspaper cuttings and action photographs and a signed log book to show somebody's been watching you all the time – evidence they can *trust*. Kate and Vicky aren't any good.'

'How do you know?'

'It says so in the front of the Guinness Book of Records. You haven't looked, have you. That just shows what a sloppy sort of record-breaker you are. *I've* read it properly. *We've* got the book at home.'

'It's lucky,' said Annabel as Julia bounced happily into the cloakroom ahead of them, 'that Julia's thick. Otherwise she wouldn't have told me yet. She'd have waited till I do break a record. That girl misses a lot of fun through being so impatient. She doesn't think ahead.'

'You *are* going to try again, then?'

'Yes, Kate. I told you, I have to.' They hung up their anoraks. 'But not in the silly way I have been doing. I was in too much of a panic.'

'What's the sensible way? What record will you go for now?'

'I don't know yet, Kate, it's going to need some cool, logical thought. But I've got an idea of the sort of thing I'm looking for. And this time it'll be properly organized *and* I'll look in the front of the book.'

That was not, however, to be so easy. During announcements in Assembly, Mr Trimm shuffled his papers and leaned an aggressive elbow on the lectern.

'Yesterday evening,' he said, 'I had complaints from people unable to post letters in the Church Lane box because of boys from this school playing the fool there and claiming they were trying to break a world record. Other boys saying the same thing were jamming themselves into the phone kiosks outside the post office and preventing people making calls.'

He sprawled menacingly over the lectern.

'I'm not a spoilsport and I can't control what you do outside the school, but I suggest that in future anybody contemplating record-breaking that involves public property should discuss it with me first. To encourage this I've removed the Guinness Book of Records from the library. Anybody wanting to consult it can come and see me.'

He relaxed. His tone mellowed.

'I understand that an attempt on the record for the world's longest daisy chain is in progress on the playing fields. This is an exciting challenge inconveniencing no one. It can continue.' Two seats in front of Kate, Fiona preened herself. 'I shall follow its progress with interest and wish its organizer, Fiona Turnbull, every success, I hope she brings this honour to the school.'

'Isn't that typical, Kate!' Annabel was cross as they left Assembly. 'My idea and now everybody else is either messing it up or getting the credit. Now I can't even look in the book. As if I'd go and ask Mr Trimm!'

'It'll be in the public library. We could go after school.'

'Oh, it doesn't matter *that* much. Julia's told me all I need to know. It's the principle.'

'But don't you need any ideas for your next record?'

'No, Kate. Not from the book, anyway.'

On that intriguing note Annabel lapsed into silent abstraction which was to remain with her for much of the school day as she presumably applied clear, logical thought. Inquiries about the onion-peeling record were turned aside with an abstracted comment that she was now after a different record, a proper one.

While Annabel sat staring into space during morning break Kate passed the time by listening to Naomi Peach at the next table. She was telling Angela Dill, Tracey Cooke and Justine Bird about her new outfit. Not from a junble sale apparently, but new, expensive and *very* exotic, all white with baggy trousers and brilliantly colourful sash and bits and bobs on it, very *oriental*, in fact, just the sort of thing Cleopatra probably wore. It would create a sensation when she wore it publicly for the first time.

This was, presumably, the outfit Naomi had been carrying in the large bag when they'd seen her in the High Street on Saturday. She'd have told Annabel all about it then, though the information hadn't been passed on to Kate. There didn't seem anything in *that* to upset Annabel. What *was* driving her on?

During dinner break Annabel roused herself a little and they went to inspect the *l-d-c-i-t-w*. Lengthy pieces of it were strewn about the playing fields waiting to be joined up.

'We're getting there,' Fiona informed them. She was in high spirits. 'A lot of teachers are coming to look at it. Mr Trimm's been along. My daisy chain's become very fashionable since he endorsed it in Assembly. I shall get the press along as soon as it's finished.'

'It's wilted,' said Annabel. 'It'll be shrivelled by the time the press get to it. Surely the point of a daisy chain is that it's not wilted.'

'I think I can smell onions,' said Fiona, pointedly. 'What happened to your record, by the way? I'd forgotten all about it. Did you think better of it?'

'Anyway,' said Annabel, ignoring the question, 'even *if* you make the longest daisy chain in the world and *if* it doesn't matter that it's shrivelled and *if* you hadn't already broken all the rules it still wouldn't count.'

'Why not?'

'Because you've got to have proper evidence all the way through. Adult witnesses and log books and things. It tells you in the front of the book but I don't suppose you've read it properly. Julia will tell you about it, I expect, but she likes to wait till you've finished, she finds it more fun that way. I'm telling you in good time so you can start again.'

'Well, I'm not starting again. My team wouldn't stand for it.'

'I was only trying to give you a friendly warning, Fiona.'

Fiona didn't want any friendly warnings. 'She doesn't,' said Annabel as they left her, 'want to face reality at all but she'll have to sooner or later.'

Annabel returned to her abstraction.

She emerged from it at the end of afternoon break when they were rising to leave the dining hall to say, quietly but decisively, 'I've got it, Kate. The right record. I've made up my mind.'

'What is it?'

'I've been looking, Kate, for a record with certain special qualities. It has to be silly or I wouldn't stand a chance but it has to have a certain dignity, too.'

'That's not an easy combination.'

'No. That's why it's taken me so long to think of it. Also, I want it to be something suitable for a public occasion, an *event* with the press present ... and a public figure ... you don't think I'm aiming too high, Kate –'

'I don't know.'

'– something *memorable*. But the most important thing of all is that it can't be an existing record, the competition for those is too hot – I know that now. I've got to be clever and set up a new one, something so silly and pointless that nobody's thought of it before yet it ought to be in the book.'

'*Are* there any?'

'I've thought of one that satisfies all those conditions, Kate.'

'What?'

'Walking backwards. I intend to become the first holder of the world's backward walking record. There was nothing in the silly ones about that, was there.'

'I don't *think* so . . . no, I'm sure there wasn't. We could check in the public library to make certain –'

'I *am* certain. I went through every one of those records. Anyway, I've remembered, it's Thursday and the library's closed all day but it couldn't matter less, Kate –'

They were now descending the stairs. Her decision made, Annabel was suddenly elated.

"The marvellous thing about this record is there's nothing to beat. I'll try as hard as I can to set up a good record, of course – I'll have to see how difficult it is before I can be sure what is a good one – but it really won't so much be *attacking* a record as *annexing* it.'

'You're sure they'll accept it?' A faint feeling that it sounded too easy was disturbing Kate.

'As long as it's a reasonable sort of performance. They've got to start their records somewhere, haven't they. It'll make their book more interesting.'

Annabel was starting to bubble. The enthusiasm was infectious . . .

'I'll try and arrange it for tomorrow evening, Kate. Have a practice session after school today. It'll be too late to catch this week's papers but something big like this will get talked about, anyway.'

. . . sweeping aside Kate's tiny doubts.

Annabel's new plan regained for her the initiative on the record-breaking scene. The first surge of unsuccessful attempts had now passed; only Fiona remained determined and her daisy chain was beginning to seem dated. Walking backwards was suddenly more fashionable.

Straight after tea Annabel went with Kate to Addendon Rec for a practice and to decide on the course. The course was easy, the perimeter track making a natural one and after an experimental backwards walk Annabel pronounced it not at all difficult.

'Might get a stiff neck after a time, Kate, that's the only thing.'

'How long do you think you could keep going? How many circuits?'

'I don't know, Kate. Just as long as I can.'

Richard White and Damian Price had strolled into the Rec to watch. Now they came over.

'What you need,' said Damian, 'is a rear view mirror. I could make you one. We've got a mirror off a moped at home. I could fix it to a headband.'

'Could you really? That would solve the stiff neck problem, wouldn't it, Kate. It would add a sort of professional touch too. Thanks, Damian.'

Richard White also had a suggestion.

'You need the Cogginton Majorettes for your record attempt. They'd make it a real occasion.'

'Never heard of them.'

'They're good, aren't they, Dame. The Twinkle-stars. They march up and down in their uniforms, twirling their batons. It's short notice but they'd do it if I asked them.'

Annabel looked suspicious and he became wheedling.

'Go on. Kirk Gregson's mum runs them and he's a friend of mine.'

'No, thanks.'

'Go on. They're always practising and nobody ever invites 'em anywhere.'

'Even more no. I want this to be a dignified occasion.'

'There are only five of them. Three are Kirk's sisters. He'd be really grateful.'

'Absolutely, definitely not.'

'You'll be missing something.'

Annabel's next move was to organize the press and a public figure. This was accomplished in one operation by calling at the Mill Lane home of councillor Mrs Winnie Stringer, who could be relied upon to grace any function if it offered publicity for herself and particularly if it involved *youth* with which she claimed a special rela-tionship and which she often described as 'our hope for the future'. She expressed great interest in the record attempt and, as Annabel had hoped, offered to contact the local press herself. The event was fixed for seven o'clock on the following evening.

'It's going to be a big occasion, isn't it, Kate,' said Annabel as they walked home. 'I've never been in anything as big as this before.' She was still elated.

There was sensational news next morning. Fiona Turnbull was in a state of shock. Mr Rumator, the groundsman, had mown the playing fields after school on the previous day, no one having informed him of the existence of the almost completed *l-d-c-i-t-w*, now sprayed into a myriad particles behind his mower. Annabel offered her sympathy 'though it *was* shrivelled, wasn't it, Fiona. Perhaps it's better it should end this way, with dignity.'

'I told you it was too grandiose, didn't I,' she said to Kate afterwards.

By morning break Fiona had recovered and was talking about the longest conga in the world. It sounded desperate. Annabel had the record-breaking field to herself again.

A sizeable crowd, mostly from Lord Willoughby's, was waiting when Annabel, in P.E. kit and carrying her rear view mirror and accompanied by Kate, arrived in the Rec at ten to seven that evening. Kate was carrying a notebook in which to keep a record of the event, to be checked and signed when completed by Mrs Stringer. There was applause and a few shouts of encouragement.

Also present were the Cogginton Majorettes, in red caps and uniforms, high-stepping up and down and twirling their batons, free hands on hips. At Annabel's approach they burst into droning song and threw their batons higher, though still cautiously, being anxious not to drop them.

> '*Rec*-ord breaker!
> *Wur*-hurld shaker!'

they sang, over and over again. No other words emerged and the tune was limited. Richard White came over, grinning.

'Good, aren't they. They made up the music themselves as well. And all free because you're a friend of mine. I couldn't keep 'em away once I'd told 'em. They're mad about getting engagements.

Annabel scowled but was distracted by the arrival of Mrs Stringer's car at the gates. With her was the local press in the shape of Len Higginson the *Advertiser*'s photographer, and the editor of the local freesheet, the *Addendon Voice*. With her customary thoroughness over publicity Mrs Stringer had picked them up on the way to make sure they came. Annabel went to greet them and lead them to the start, a chalk line across the path.

Kate noticed that Annabel was continually glancing about her as if perhaps hoping to see someone in particular among the spectators.

Probably though, she was merely surveying her audience and she could hardly have wished for a better turnout. They came from all years at Willers. Miles Noggins was tensely popping smarties into his mouth, keenly anticipating, just as if he were at a real world event. Fiona Turnbull stood with arms folded and the slightly cynical air of an insider. A few people out walking their dogs had stopped to look. Julia Channing was just coming in through the gate carrying the Guinness Book of Records under her arm. Kate found that faintly disturbing.

Annabel donned her rear view mirror, producing more applause. The mirror was attached, by means of a length of copper tubing, to a kind of coronet – in real life a plant pot holder – which fitted over her head and projected forward like an antenna. Annabel had been thrilled with it when first trying it on, pronouncing it 'very clever'. Kate was less sure about it.

Mrs Stringer delivered a short speech, most of it drowned, to her obvious annoyance, by the Cogginton Majorettes droning and high-stepping just behind her. Kate caught various key phrases '. . . nothing wrong with the youth of today . . . too often criticized . . . more mature and intelligent than my generation' – placing an approving hand on the shoulder of Annabel, who was adjusting her rear view mirror, which was slipping – 'thrilling challenge . . . make the name of Addendon ring round the world . . .'

Annabel took up her place with her back to the

chalk line. The Cogginton Majorettes worked themselves into a frenzy, hurling knees and batons still higher and more raggedly, intensifying still further the noise level of their song.

'R-e-e-e-cord breaker!
Wur-*hur*-hurld shaker!'

'Ready!' cried Mrs Stringer. 'Steady! Go!' To cheers and two camera flashes Annabel stepped briskly backwards and the world record annexation had begun.

Annabel immediately walked crabwise into the spectators and the rear view mirror fell off. 'Sorry,' she said to the world at large, 'I'll start again.'

She stooped to pick it up but Julia Channing was already doing so.

'What are you doing?' asked Julia, handing it to her.

'What's it look as if I'm doing?' retorted Annabel, removing the coronet which had remained on her head. The mirror had only been jammed into the copper tubing and needed jamming back. 'I'm setting up a world record for walking backwards.'

'That's what somebody said but I didn't believe it. Do you know what the record stands at?'

'There isn't a record.' Annabel pushed the threaded end of the mirror holder into the tubing. 'I'm the first to try.'

'Are you ready, Annabel?' called Mrs Stringer, a little impatiently.

'Yes, there *is* a record.'

'No, there isn't.' Slow hand-clapping was starting. Annabel replaced the coronet on her head and took a sighting in the mirror. 'We looked at all the silly ones.'

'This isn't a silly one.' Julia produced the Guinness Book of Records from under her arm and opened it at a place marked by a strip of paper. 'Page 332, Sports, Games and Pastimes. You didn't look properly again, did you. You're always so impetuous.'

Annabel, about to return to the start, halted.

'What is it?'

Some of the spectators were pushing at Julia, trying to look at the Guinness Book of Records over her shoulder. She pushed back.

'It's held by somebody called Mr Flennie L. Wingo. Unusual name, isn't it? He set it up in 1932 which is quite a long time ago and it's from Santa Monica, California to Turkey.'

'Turkey, California?'

'No, just Turkey.'

'Not – where the Delight comes from. Ankara . . . Istanbul?'

'Istanbul is where he finished his backwards walk. That was about 8000 miles. How much did you have in mind?'

Annabel looked at Addendon Rec. The slow hand-clapping was increasing in volume and there was a chant of 'Why are we waiting?'

'But . . . *why*? There wasn't even a Guinness Book of Records in those days.'

'Perhaps,' said Julia, 'he wanted to make his mark. Or impress his girl-friend. I don't know, do I? *And* I expect he did it without the help of a rear view mirror. Mind you, I can see his point. He wouldn't want to look stupid right across America and Europe, would he.'

Her gleeful cackle, hitherto restrained with great effort, burst out in splendour. 'Perhaps you should go in the Guinness Book of Records as the world's sloppiest record-breaker.'

'Annabel!' called Mrs Stringer crossly, 'what's wrong?'

The rear view mirror holder suddenly turned in the tubing and the mirror swung downwards to dangle in front of Annabel's face. She blew at it despairingly.

'Everything, I'm afraid, Mrs Stringer.'

The Cogginton Majorettes, preoccupied with their own affairs – for, after all, they had marks of their own to make – continued relentlessly to sing:

> '*Reck*-ud breaker!
> *Wurr*-hurld shaker!'

hurling their batons splendidly the while.

And yet, from this débâcle, this seething cauldron of humiliation, Annabel was to rise phoenix-like almost immediately. When she dashed from the

Rec after a hurried and apologetic statement that the annexation had to be called off because of unforeseen circumstances it was not to flee to the privacy of her bedroom, there to burst into tears, but to get to the public library before it closed.

Kate, having followed her with difficulty, found her in the reference department with the Guinness Book of Records open on the table in front of her.

'This time, Kate, I'm going to read this book from cover to cover. Who printed it, conditions of sale, everything.'

'Annabel, not again, surely! It seems as least as hard making your mark through the Guinness Book of Records as any other way. Harder, if you ask me.'

But all Annabel would say was: 'Don't distract me, Kate. You don't seem to realize. It's Saturday tomorrow. *Saturday!*'

And by the following morning she was once more reaching for the stars.

Chapter 4

*****

At ten to nine next morning Annabel returned to the Rec, this time at the head of a small retinue. She was, curiously, in her best dress – light blue cotton with purple leaves on it – and carrying her violin in its case.

Behind her, Kate and Vicky Pearce walked side by side, Kate carrying a suitcase and music stand and Vicky a kitchen chair. Julian Parlane followed with two cameras, cine and still, and a tripod while bringing up the rear, somewhat sheepishly, was Kate's father bearing three deckchairs. Sticking out of his pocket was the notebook which Kate had intended to use for a log on the previous evening.

Annabel stopped in front of the fountain which stood at an intersection of paths near where the cricket ground adjoined the Rec, only a short distance from the back of the sports pavilion.

'Here,' she said and put her violin case down.

'Pretty silly place,' grumbled Kate's father. He looked embarrassed, nevertheless he started to unfold the deckchairs. Vicky placed the kitchen chair on a spot indicated by Annabel and Kate stood the suitcase on it, then positioned the music stand carefully in front of it. Some boys who had been kicking a football about gathered round to watch.

Annabel opened the suitcase and took from it a pile of violin music, mostly easy pieces for beginners, which she arranged on the stand, then a card in a wooden holder upon which was carefully printed, in block capitals:

WORLD RECORD ATTEMPT
VIOLIN PLAYING ENDURANCE

This she placed on the path beside the chair. She then removed the suitcase from the chair, took her violin from its case, sat down, smoothed her dress and composed herself, ready to play. She made, Kate thought, rather a pretty picture in the sunshine with the fountain for a background. Was she aware of this herself? Perhaps she was.

'Better than onion-peeling, isn't it, Kate,' she commented, a little self-consciously.

At ten seconds to nine o'clock by Mr Stocks' watch she raised her bow to the playing position and at nine precisely, with Julian Parlane recording the event on his cine-camera, swept into the first wavering notes of *Valse Triste*. Annabel's third attempt to establish a world record was under way.

And this, she had said, was the final one. This was IT.

The boys returned to their football.

The weather for the record attempt was fine with some sunshine and scattered cloud, no breeze, temperature at 9 a.m. of 16 degrees celsius, 61 fahrenheit. The forecast promised some further sunshine during the morning but thickening cloud and showers moving in from the west during the afternoon.

It had been, for Annabel, a thrilling discovery that there was, in the Guinness Book of Records, no violin endurance record. For piano playing, yes. But none for an instrument as important as the violin. *Her* instrument! The one she played in the school orchestra! And she had checked and rechecked. Julia couldn't catch her out this time. And what a lovely, romantic record! There could be none better.

She had recruited Julian Parlane, brainiest boy in 3 G, to take the pictures – which he was keen to do, photography being a hobby of his – borrowing ahead on her pocket money to pay for the film. If the attempt were successful, and this time there could surely be no doubt for this was definitely unspoken for, 'up for grabs' as some might say, the *Advertiser* would certainly print one and probably other papers, too.

She had also persuaded Kate's father – to Kate's admiring astonishment – to attend as adult witness and keep the log book, though he now seemed to be regretting this.

Vicky Pearce had insisted upon coming along as a witness, too, having become contrite over her performance at the onion-peeling attempt and anxious to redeem herself. Annabel had been too soft-hearted to tell her that she wasn't needed on this occasion.

'*This* is *my* record, Kate,' Annabel had said, 'the one I feel at home with, the one I was destined for. The others were just silly false starts.'

Perhaps. And perhaps it was understandable that she should wear her best dress for such a momentous occasion. But why, wondered Kate, here in the Rec? Especially when you considered those clouds moving in from the west. Annabel hadn't explained that. But why?

Mr Stocks sat in a deckchair and read a newspaper. Vicky Pearce sat in another and painted her nails blue. Kate, in the third, read an Agatha Christie. Julian Parlane prowled around looking for fresh angles. Passers-by paused to stare and an old lady peered short-sightedly then dropped a tenpenny piece in front of Annabel which Mr Stocks insisted on giving back to her. A mother wheeling a pram stopped then moved quickly on again rocking the pram and making chattering faces when the baby howled.

Annabel's violin wavered on, sometimes melancholy, sometimes sprightly. *Annie Laurie, Poor Old Joe*, something Spanish, something Russian, back to *Valse Triste*. At a quarter to ten a football rolled under her chair and the boys came crowding round wanting it back. Mr Stocks chased them away and booted the ball after them bad-temperedly.

At ten, Annabel paused for her first five

minutes rest period (this time she knew the rules and that she was entitled to one of these per hour) and to drink some orange juice. Mr Stocks made a note of this in the log book, not knowing what else to put in it. She resumed with renewed vigour.

She was, she commented, feeling better now than at the beginning. And already the solid practice was improving her playing. Did everyone notice what a lilt she was getting into the *Humoresque*? She felt as if she could go on forever. Mr Stocks looked unhappy at this. He had assumed, when agreeing to his role, that Annabel would only last for an hour or two although she had told him that she intended to play all day, at least until it got dark.

'I may not be able to approach the piano-playing record,' she had said, 'which if I remember rightly is something like seven weeks, but I can try to do something decent.'

Vicky Pearce, bored by the blue nail varnish, began to remove it. Kate made her first tentative guess at the murderer's identity.

At twenty past ten Annabel's mother turned up with a flask of tea and biscuits and to check that everything was all right and Annabel wasn't making a nuisance of herself. After a chat with Mr Stocks she left satisfied. Kate fed some of the biscuits to Annabel while she played.

Largo from the *New World Symphony* . . . *Bluebells of Scotland* . . . *Battle Hymn of the Republic* . . . a dog sniffed around Annabel then went away. For want of anything better to do, Mr Stocks wrote that up in the log book, too, before closing his eyes. He'd finished the newspaper.

Danse Macabre . . . Valse Triste . . . Home Sweet Home . . . Poor Old Joe . . .

The eleven o'clock break came and went. Vicky Pearce painted her nails black, Kate changed her mind about the murderer. During the twelve o'clock break, having first asked Kate to make sure the pavilion was open, Annabel sprinted there for a reviving wash and tidy-up, racing back with face and hands dripping saying she hadn't had time to dry herself.

At 12.15 Mr Stocks rose, yawning, saying he deserved a break himself and was going to stretch his legs. He would trust Kate, Julian and Vicky to deputize in his absence, keeping up the log, and would expect a full report on his return. Annabel, without looking away from the music, protested that this might be against the rules and he ought to stay there all the time. He replied that as a responsible adult he could surely be relied upon to know when to delegate and went off, leaving the log book and biro with Kate. By lunch time he still hadn't returned.

Julian Parlane went home at ten to one, promising to return later. He had spent most of the morning doing homework, breaking off to take pictures with either of his cameras whenever he noticed a change of background or cloud conditions. He said that the position of shadows would show that Annabel had been there all day. Vicky

Pearce said she might simply have moved her chair round the fountain but Kate replied that wouldn't work. It gave them something to talk about for ten minutes.

Annabel was by now becoming glassy-eyed and the music had deteriorated into squeals and scrapings. A lunch of chicken and ham pie, hard-boiled egg and tea, gobbled during the one o'clock break, revived her and *Danse Macabre* was quite spirited when she resumed. Kate wrote up the details of Annabel's lunch while she and Vicky ate picnics on the grass.

Mr Stocks reappeared at 1.25 looking well-fed and contented and carrying a portable radio. After riffling through the log book and congratulating Kate upon her entries he settled down to listen to some music, keeping the volume low so as not to annoy anyone, though it annoyed Annabel who considered it a reflection on her playing. Shortly afterwards, Vicky Pearce went home briefly, re-appearing just after the two o'clock break with a cassette recorder which she plugged into her ears pretending not to notice Annabel's long look. Kate was back with her Agatha Christie.

Au clair de la lune . . . *What Sweet Content* by Bach . . . *Jingle Bells* . . .

At 2.20 the promised cloud moved in from the west, the sun disappeared and it began to drizzle. Mr Stocks noted this in the log and asked if Annabel wanted to give up now. She replied that of course she didn't. There was a selection of rainwear in the suitcase if Kate would be kind enough to get it out.

Kate and Vicky put on anoraks while Mr Stocks unenthusiastically donned sailing gear which he had allowed to be brought without seriously expecting to have to use it. Annabel declined an anorak, saying it would interfere with her playing. For her there was an umbrella which would also protect the violin. Kate tied it to the back of her chair with string.

Certainly, thought Kate, the effect was strangely pleasing, Annabel making a still prettier picture now in her umbrella-capped chair, like a fairy fiddler beneath a toadstool, solemn, intent, leaning tenderly into her violin, somehow remote from and above the ordinariness of the Rec, now deserted under grey, drizzling skies save for the huddled, morose figures of the invigilators in their deckchairs.

Ethereal was the word, perhaps.

What had been forgotten, though, as Annabel soon pointed out, was protection for the music. It was getting wet. Glad to have something to do – for reading in the rain held no attraction and she had set the Agatha Christie aside – Kate volunteered to dash home for another umbrella and something to fix it to.

Hurrying along the High Street she heard music and saw some seven or eight Lord Willoughby's boys and girls playing the fool outside the post office, shuffling around in a sort of chain and chanting. They included Tracey Cooke and

Edward Chance and when the chain turned she saw that its leader was Fiona Turnbull carrying a cassette recorder. It dawned upon her that this was the longest conga in the world.

Sic transit gloria murmured Annabel when Kate arrived back with the umbrella and a folding garden chair and more string and told her about it. The last of her potential rivals had finally been seen off. The news put fresh life into her playing, which had been flagging again. She went into something jauntily Irish.

At ten past three Julian Parlane returned to take more pictures against the background of the changed weather conditions. He seemed delighted to have the opportunity, even more so when at about 3.25 the drizzle turned to steady rain from a dark sky. He thought the pictures would be quite dramatic and went home intending to ask his father if he might use his dark-room and equipment to develop them. He wouldn't, alas, be able to take any more. He'd used all the film and, anyway, wouldn't be allowed to have the cameras again. Apparently they were both extremely valuable and belonged to his father.

Vicky Pearce left at this time, too, complaining that she didn't feel she was being much use, certainly not enough to catch pneumonia for, though she might come back later.

Kate's father, meanwhile, was growing irritable. There was no longer any music on the radio to his taste and he had turned it off. Now he and Annabel began to bicker.

'It's ridiculous staying out here. If you're not going to stop then at least move indoors. You could go home.'

'I can't. I'd have to stop playing.'

'You could play walking along. I'll hold the umbrella. Or I'll drive you home. You could play in the car.'

Annabel refused. Kate walked damply up and down with hunched shoulders licking the rain-water off her lips. Her father muttered and snarled.

'That's a good kitchen chair you're sitting on. It'll warp.'

'It's under the umbrella, Mr Stocks.'

On and on and on . . . *Mazurka* by Tchaikovsky . . . *Twinkle, Twinkle, Little Star* . . . *Valse Triste* . . .

At ten to four Annabel's mother reappeared with another flask of tea and expressed surprise and concern that they were still out there. She'd assumed they'd have moved under cover some-where and seemed to feel that Mr Stocks was to blame for the fact that they hadn't. She didn't want Annabel catching cold nor – with an aggrieved glance at Kate's father – did she want the chair to warp.

The situation might have become awkward if the rain hadn't stopped then, just in time for the four o'clock break. While Annabel drank her tea and flexed the fingers of her left hand Mrs

Bunce rubbed a handkerchief over the chair. She went home saying that Annabel could stay but ought to find shelter if it started raining again.

Vicky Pearce returned with the drier weather but after hovering around for a few minutes finally left again saying that nobody seemed to care if she were there or not anyway. No one commented.

At 4.35 Mr Stocks changed his tactics to jovial wheedling. 'Seven and a half hours is pretty good, isn't it. Not a bad record at all. Why not settle for that? You said yourself there isn't any competition.'

'But there might be. I want my record to stand for at least a little while, Mr Stocks.' At five o'clock, Annabel dashed off for another spruce-up and came back dripping again.

Santa Lucia . . . Brahms' *Cradle Song* . . . *Poor Old Joe* . . . On and on and on and on . . . Afternoon became evening. Although the steady rain didn't return there were occasional little flurries blown on the gusty little breeze that had got up and the skies remained a gloomy grey. Annabel's expression moved from the steadfast to the strained to the suffering. Her bowing became more saw-like, the music more slurred and wandering. Kate's father sat slumped and motionless.

On and on and on . . .

'Why *here*?' wondered Kate.

*

At about half past seven there was a surge of activity in the Rec as a steady stream of young men and girls came along the path past the fountain making for the sports pavilion. Amongst them, Kate noticed, were several seniors from Lord Willoughby's. All were dressed as for a party and virtually all did a double-take and hesitated when they saw Annabel before moving on, usually chuckling, to continue round the side of the pavilion to the entrance, which was at the front. Kate's father slumped still lower and pretended he was asleep.

At about the same time lights went on in the pavilion and the steady thump of music started up. To Kate, pacing up and down trying to keep warm, it looked alluringly jolly and inviting. Darkness was falling prematurely because of the low cloud and raindrops were blowing off the trees.

'Must be a party in the pavilion,' she said, pausing by Annabel. 'Is it the start of the cricket season or something?'

'It might be, I suppose,' replied Annabel. 'I don't really know, Kate.' Although she wasn't betraying any interest Kate noticed that her playing had sharpened up again and her face had relinquished its suffering expression and become alert. She was into *Valse Triste* once more.

The activity across the Rec was dying down when a spectacular figure came in through the gates; someone in a white, baggy-trousered outfit with a brilliant red sash and other colourful bits and bobs, the whole seeming to illuminate the Rec with its glow. Some mighty queen of old Baghdad, perhaps, or ancient Egypt? Cleopatra herself, risen again?

'It's Naomi Peach,' said Kate, watching the figure approach. 'What's *she* doing here? In *that*?' Naomi had not been unduly boastful. Her new outfit was truly sensational.

Annabel made no reply. She was concentrating upon her music, drawing upon her almost exhausted resources to produce her finest rendering yet of *Valse Triste*.

Naomi halted in front of her. She had been the last person to enter the Rec. No one had followed.

'Like it?' she asked, referring to her outfit, beside which the fact that Annabel was sitting in the cold and semi-darkness playing the violin was hardly worth noticing.

Annabel awarded her the briefest of squints.

'It's very nice.'

Naomi smiled the smile of one totally certain of herself.

'I suppose this is some record you're after. Hope you get it.'

This showed magnanimity after Annabel's offhandedness. She started to move on.

'Where are you going, Naomi?' Kate asked. 'What's happening in the pavilion?'

'Haven't you heard? It's a party for Andrew Torrance. In honour of him being the youngest boy ever to be made reserve for the county cricket team.' She smiled, dazzlingly. 'He invited me himself. I'm the only person from the Third Year coming.'

A screech from the violin suddenly made clear to Kate much that had puzzled her.

'*Andrew Torrance*! But why's he invited *you*?'

'That's rather rudely put but I suppose it's because of my position as *Their Lordships'* Fan Club secretary and the piece about me in the paper. I think there's a general feeling that I'm someone now. I'm part of the Addendon establishment. I've made my mark.'

There was a spatter of raindrops from the trees.

'I'm going in,' said Naomi, hastily. 'Don't want to get wet. Sooner you than me out here. It's a funny place to set up a record.'

The noise from the pavilion had swelled. A murmur of voices and laughter was now mixed with the music which, Kate realized, was being provided by *Their Lordships*. She hadn't seen them pass this way so presumably they'd approached the pavilion from the other direction. Yes, of course; from the pavilion car park. They'd have come in the old camping van they travelled around in.

More importantly, Andrew Torrance must have approached from that direction too because he hadn't come through the Rec either and it was unlikely he'd be late for a party in his honour.

Annabel must have realized that, too, realized it well before Kate probably without at first being willing to admit it to herself. Her head was sinking, her playing listless again. The traffic through the Rec had ceased.

Kate knew now why Annabel had chosen this spot and why she was wearing her best dress. She had known about the party; had no doubt learned of it from Naomi a week ago in the High Street; it was what had suddenly silenced her. She had expected Andrew Torrance to pass this way and see her and be left in no doubt that, if not yet actually in the record books, she was on the brink of being someone too, virtually a part of the Addendon establishment.

Her reasons for wanting to make her mark had nothing to do with Auntie Lucy Loxby or Mozart. She just wanted to be invited to Andrew Torrance's party. As long as he'd never much noticed anyone else from the Third Year his ignorance of her existence had been perfectly tolerable. Now he'd noticed Naomi it was not and no plan to rectify the situation was too wild and desperate.

But she had guessed wrongly. He hadn't come to the party this way. Her face was buried in the violin.

Kate's father suddenly shuddered and rose stiffly to his feet.

'Surely that's enough. You've done –' he glanced at his watch '– ten hours, fifty-four minutes. I didn't expect you to do a quarter of that. Come on. It's getting dark.'

The strongest little gust of wind yet riffled the pages of her music and Kate went to hold them down though Annabel was mostly playing from memory now anyway. The trees shed more raindrops and from Annabel came a sound which might have been a cough or perhaps a sob.

There was a sudden temporary increase in the noise level as the pavilion door opened and closed. In the gathering gloom, three figures appeared round the corner.

'There's Andrew Torrance,' said Kate, 'with two other boys. They're looking at you.'

They must have heard about the strange figure in the Rec and come to see for themselves. Were they laughing at her? It was too dark to tell. Their faces were in shadow.

Annabel did not reply or look up. She was playing a simple Hebridean folk-song now, something slow and yearning that, even under her inexperienced bow, pulled at the soul, drawing it to things that are wild and lost and beautiful, things that are perhaps no more save in the imagination of such as Annabel because they are too delicate and romantic, too tender and poignant and private for this rough-riding world. Annabel's head remained bowed and a droplet that looked like rain but was not lay upon her cheek. She was playing as Kate had never heard her play before, pouring all her passion into the wind and the raindrops and the darkness as she had never done for school orchestra because Andrew Torrance was listening and perhaps he, too, knew about those wild, lost beautiful things.

The melody came to an end and she stopped and

lowered the violin and bow to her lap and sat with downcast eyes. The time was eight o'clock precisely.

'That's it, Mr Stocks,' she whispered. 'That's my record. Would you care to note the time in the log and sign it and perhaps Kate will sign it too.'

'Thank goodness for that!' he said and climbed stiffly to his feet. Kate suddenly tugged at his sleeve, pulling him away. Though puzzled, he made no resistance.

Andrew Torrance had left his friends and was walking towards Annabel. As he came out of the deeper shadow of the pavilion and trees Kate saw that he was not laughing.

Annabel remained motionless, head bowed, seemingly numb and exhausted, oblivious to the world. Kate continued to draw her father away and he, realizing now that something of moment was happening, co-operated.

Andrew Torrance had halted in front of Annabel, was saying something to her. She was lifting her eyes to look at him, replying, perhaps answering questions about her record or about the music, now glancing about her, apparently looking to see where Kate and her father had got to, at the same time saying something else. Kate was able to lip-read it:

'Can my friend Kate come too?'

She had been invited to the party. She was rising now, beckoning Kate, looking not at all numb or exhausted but enchanted for she had made her mark and had been noticed by Andrew

Torrance. It may be that by tomorrow morning he would have forgotten her again but that didn't matter. For this evening and therefore for always she would be part of his experience. Even if only in some remote recess of his subconscious they would share forever his party and the yearning ache of a Hebridean folk-song played in a gusting little wind amid the spatter of raindrops.

Yet in this moment of moments, Annabel had not forgotten Kate, her best friend. And he was nodding, turning away, obviously suggesting they follow.

Kate wasn't dressed for a party but that didn't matter. She could tidy up in the pavilion. All that needed to be done was dispose of the impedimenta of record-breaking and her father was only too eager to attend to that. It was, he assured them, what he'd been looking forward to all day. Yes, yes, Kate could go to the party and he'd ring Annabel's parents to tell them where she was.

They left him enthusiastically collecting up the deckchairs to take to his car and made for the pavilion, Annabel still enchanted for the stars were within her grasp.

Someone was approaching, coming out of the gloom of the Rec behind a large umbrella. It lifted to reveal Julia Channing carrying the Guinness Book of Records. She had just taken it from her shoulder bag, the flap of which was back revealing the top of a vacuum flask inside. Had Julia been picnicking? Alone in the rain? In the Rec? She was giggling sillily, though fighting against it.

'Lo, Annabel,' she said, 'I was just passing. Is it true what I've heard, that you've been having a go at another record? Violin playing, somebody said.'

'Yes, Julia, I've just finished, as it happens.'

'How long did you play?'

'Eleven hours.'

'Oh dear! You make me feel guilty Annabel because I should really have mentioned this earlier but I did think you'd know the rules by now.' Despite her efforts, Julia's giggle became even sillier as she opened the book, seeking a page. 'I'm afraid it says here in the foreword that they're –' she adopted a reading voice '– "inclined to publish only those records which improve upon previous records or which are newly significant in having become the subject of widespread and preferably international competitiveness". I don't think violin playing comes under either of those two categories, does it, Annabel. What they're saying is the book's full up and they don't want any more unless they're really important ones. It's a terrible tragedy Annabel and I do feel mean to be the one to have to bring the news but you've been wasting your time.'

'It's kind of you to take the trouble to come and tell me, Julia,' said Annabel. 'I can't tell you how much I appreciate it. But you needn't have bothered. I read that.'

Julia got her giggle under control at last. 'You read it?'

'Yes, Julia.'

About to move on, Annabel changed her mind

and paused again. On an evening such as this she did not wish to be unkind to any fellow human being, even Julia. And if, as was to be assumed, Julia had spent a wet Saturday hiding in the Rec with packed lunch and vacuum flask waiting to savour this moment it must be a wretched anti-climax for her. In common decency some sort of explanation was owed even if it left aside those aspects which Julia could not be expected to understand, for of course it was probably outside her mental capacity to appreciate that there might be more reasons for attempting a world record than merely wanting to establish a world record.

'You see, Julia, they don't say they *won't* accept any new records, just that they're not *inclined* to. It's up to the Guinness Book of Records people to decide, of course, but perhaps when I've pointed out to them what a very important instrument the violin is they may feel they can allow it.

'Anyway, I shall send it up to them and see. I'll tell them I don't want to argue or discuss it, I shall just look in the Guinness Book of Records next year and see if my name's there. I think it ought to be. Frankly, my opinion of them will be lower if it isn't. But it's their decision. It's up to them and if it goes against me I shall understand.'

With eyes lifted to where the stars should be, Annabel entered the pavilion.

FIGHTING IN BREAK AND OTHER STORIES

Edited by Barbara Ireson

What if you don't want to fight? What if you've stolen another boy's balaclava and want to give it back but don't dare? And what do you do when your mother makes you take a bright blue bag to school when everyone else's is greeny-brown? Here is a collection of twelve stories about school by such well-known writers as Robin Klein, Margaret Joy, Sylvia Woods and many more.

THE BIG PINK

Ann Pilling

Straight from her friendly local comprehensive, Angela is plunged into the alien life of her aunt's boarding school for girls. Overweight and horribly self-conscious, she immediately attracts the disapproval of Auntie Pat and the suspicions of the girls in her dormitory. But she finds allies in the school's more colourful characters, and her secret talent wins her the admiration of Sebastian, the teenage grandson of the school's benefactor. But still nothing she does will please Auntie Pat!

MAGGIE AND ME

Ted Staunton

Maggie's always got some brilliant plan – and Cyril inevitably has to help her. Whether it's getting back at the school bully or swapping places for piano lessons, these best friends are forever having adventures. Poor Cyril! Life without Maggie would be an awful lot easier, but then it would be much more boring. What would he do if she ever moved away? Here are ten stories about the intrepid duo.

FRYING AS USUAL
Joan Lingard

Disaster strikes the Francettis when Mr Francetti breaks his leg. Their fish and chip shop never closes, but who is going to run it now that he's in hospital, and their mother is in Italy? The answer is quite simple to Toni, Rosita and Paula, and with the help of Grandpa they decide to carry on frying as usual. But it's not that easy . . .

THE FREEDOM MACHINE
Joan Lingard

Mungo dislikes Aunt Janet and to avoid staying with her he decides to hit the open road and look after himself, and with his bike he heads northwards bound for adventure and freedom. But he soon discovers that freedom isn't quite what he'd expected, especially when his food supplies are stolen, and in the course of his journey he learns a few things about himself.

KING DEATH'S GARDEN
Ann Halam

Maurice has discovered a way of visiting the past, and whatever its dangers it's too exciting for him to want to give up – yet. A subtle and intriguing ghost story for older readers.